An orange bouncing slightly a stop against his shoe. He glanced down, then refocused on the slender girl wearing a flowered dress and low-heeled shoes as she slowly straightened, a tomato in each hand. Dry spaghetti noodles still lay scattered on the sidewalk. Furrowed brows scrunched over stormy eyes told how she felt about the ripped bag and her food landing on the cement.

Aching muscles from cramped airplane seating were forgotten as he watched dark hair swing forward to shield her face when she squatted again to corral more vegetables. Without taking time to analyze the increased thumping inside his chest, he set down his luggage and reached for the orange before closing the distance between them. Not waiting for permission to help, he knelt on one knee and began to gather the sticks of dried pasta. She rose and took a step back, drawing his gaze up to meet hers.

Un colpo di Fulmine.

As the thought struck, actual words stuck in a suddenly-dry throat. He swallowed once, then again. Without breaking eye contact, he slowly rose, holding the spaghetti in one hand like a bunch of flowers. Now what?

Something about the whole scene drew out a soft chuckle. "Um, sorry." He leaned to pick up the ripped bag and wrapped it around the noodles then glanced toward the boardinghouse before reconnecting with her gaze. "I'm here to see Hannah Montgomery."

Her smile gradually appeared and eventually reached her eyes. "I'm Hannah."

Praise for Sandra McGregor

"Cinderella meets Pearl Harbor! Loved this story [*EMMA ROSE*] and the amazing feelings Emma and Thomas brought out in me. The connection between the characters was perfect. I was rooting for these two the whole story! I would recommend to everyone who loves an amazing love story that has the power to move you like a Nicolas Sparks book."

When Truth Takes Flight

by

Sandra McGregor

When Truth Takes Flight

Cover Art by *Tina Lynn Stout*

The Wild Rose Press, Inc.
PO Box 708
Adams Basin, NY 14410-0708
Visit us at www.thewildrosepress.com

Publishing History
First Vintage Rose Edition, 2017
Print ISBN 978-1-5092-1866-0
Digital ISBN 978-1-5092-1867-7

Published in the United States of America

Dedication

Thanks to my editor, Stacy D. Holmes.
You make my stories better.
~*~
Also, to my Lake Sisters
(you know who you are).
I appreciate your encouragement, input,
and most of all, your friendship.

Chapter One

New York City looked different after ten years. More cars, more people, more filth. Nothing new about that. With the Great War fading into history and the country rebounding slowly from depression, John Staples knew times were changing for the better. Especially for him. With college in his rear-view mirror, the next step was to secure a job, but first, he needed to take care of an obligation.

While the cab driver tossed his small case on the front seat of the red and yellow Skyline and then trotted around to slide in behind the steering wheel, John climbed into the backseat and sat at a slight angle to allow his long legs an extra couple inches. The mid-day sun beat down on the car's roof, intensifying the pungent odor of stale cigars and sweat. He wrinkled his nose at the thought of prior passengers, while sweat beaded on his forehead, trickled down the sides of his face, and plastered the starched white shirt to his body. It brought back recent memories of the sauna in the men's locker room at college.

After a relatively mild May, June had arrived with sweltering temperatures that now blistered the Eastern seaboard. The city was melting, leaving everyone limp and listless. At least his home state of Alabama had been blessed with an ocean breeze off the Gulf for the past several days. He'd left that cool reprieve in Mobile when he boarded the plane headed north.

With hardly a forethought, he reached up and loosened his tie, then hesitated, mentally fighting the urge to remove the noose and suit jacket. No. He needed to be prepared for whatever waited for him at the hotel. His lips quirked up to one side as he pondered the thought of a suit and tie being armor against someone like Vince.

"Where to, buddy?" The driver slammed the car door and glanced in the rear-view mirror, talking around a wad of gum he continued to maul while he waited.

He guessed the man was easily twice his age—old enough to be his father and probably old enough to have seen action in the war. "The Ritz."

With a quick nod, the driver fired up the engine, cranked the large steering wheel to the left, and with the barest glance over his shoulder, stomped on the gas pedal to send the car darting into the flow of traffic. John tensed, his right foot slamming down on the floor as if his effort could keep them out of harm's way. Horns blared, but the cab managed to slip between another bright yellow taxi and a passenger car without incident.

"Crazy drivers," the string-thin man mumbled, his flashed grin prominently displaying teeth tarnished from years of smoking. "They all think they own the road."

John nodded without comment, leaving the man to shrug bony shoulders and focus on the road. He slowly relaxed his foot, and his heartbeat gradually returned to normal while he pictured the '34 coupe being reduced to scrap metal. The deep sigh was silent, but blown upward to ruffle the hair that drooped across his sweat-drenched forehead. The hot air blowing through the open window added exhaust fumes and only circulated the heat.

More uncomfortable than he'd been in some time, he lifted a hand to remove the offending tie, but hesitated again. Instead, he leaned to the side, reached into a back pocket, and retrieved the handkerchief to wipe his face. It might be early June, but the oppressive heat squeezed his lungs while he labored to suck in the exhaust-filled air held at street level by towering brick buildings that lined the streets like prison walls.

To his right, a car horn blasted, drowning out the words that accompanied the hand gestures. He'd never understand the hurry—the constant jostling to advance a few inches in the overwhelming congestion.

He cringed slightly as the cab narrowly missed a young man on a bicycle. Horns blared, but the rider escaped. The traffic slowed and became more congested, sure signs they'd soon be in the center of the city—and arriving at the meeting he'd been anticipating, yet dreading, for longer than he cared to think about.

Vince Giovanni.

The name conjured up memories of the only man to ever take time to play catch with him—the man whose picture had made the front page of the *Times* on numerous occasions. John wasn't sure what to expect, but if the letter of congratulation for graduating college with an engineering degree was any indication, the meeting would be friendly. Actually, he figured there was little reason for Vince to hold the past against him, but, according to his mother, there was every reason for the older man to summon him to New York under the pretense of celebrating. Of course, if his mother's warnings were accurate, it might prove to be a very long and uncomfortable afternoon.

This time, his sigh sounded like a soft groan and drew the cabby's attention.

"Long trip?"

"Just a few hours."

"First time in New York?"

This wasn't the time for small talk, nor was he in the mood. There was too much on his mind.

"It's been a while," he muttered, allowing his head to relax back against the seat and his eyelids to close. When no further questions were forthcoming, he dismissed the driver, assuming the man would deliver him safely to the Ritz-Carlton, leaving him time to replay the earlier conversation with his mother...

Her words had stabbed—harsh and gritty with emotion while her tear-filled eyes blazed.

"Don't be naïve. Once Vince gets you up there, he'll move heaven and earth to keep you there. He'll promise you the moon—and a few stars for good measure," she added, making a motion with her hand to imitate something rolling on and on. "You'll think you've grabbed the brass ring, but it won't take you long to realize what you really have is a ring in your nose, and you're being fed crumbs while he spends his time and energy on his...his *job*."

John had felt the full gale force of his mother's tirade. Red-haired people were known for their tempers and, at that moment, she fit the stereotype. He'd held off as long as possible before telling her about the invitation to fly to New York, knowing she would lose her temper at the very mention of his stepfather's name. He'd also known there would be hell to pay when he told her his decision to accept the invitation.

"Mother, he paid for my college. He just wants to celebrate with me—dinner, maybe a stage show. That's it. Why are you so upset? You're acting like I'm going up there to join his organization or something." His chuckle only made her glare harden. Like a statue cut from stone, her face had been cold and unyielding.

Hands jammed on slightly-widened hips, she'd narrowed her gaze, pinning him where he stood. His mother being angry as a wet hen was nothing new, but something had been different about this confrontation. The subject of her former husband historically caused irritation, but not the level of desperation that had radiated from her at that moment. Had the reaction really been anger, or fear?

Why would she ever fear Vince?

"Why in the world would you feel an obligation to fly to New York City and rub shoulders with a criminal?" she'd continued. "The whole idea is crazy."

He remained silent, not knowing how to answer without making the situation worse.

Her temper eased a bit. "Johnny," she said, relaxing her shoulders and allowing her arms to lower to her sides, "I'm proud of you—you know that, right?" When he nodded, she continued, "Well, I won't dispute that you're educated and intelligent, but book learning won't help you in dealing with thugs."

Her breaths became faster again, working up to another temper—and there'd been nothing he could do to prevent it, but stand a bit taller and brace for impact.

"You're a college graduate, but you don't know

everything. You don't know Vince—at least not the way I know him."

"Mother…"

"He abandoned his first wife while she was pregnant with his child. He just divorced her and kicked her out." She'd reached out to grasp his arm, her eyes stormy, but taking on an edge of pleading. "What kind of man does such a thing?"

He'd never heard any of this before. His mother's statement made no sense. "So, why did you marry him?"

She wilted before his eyes, her focus on the scuffed linoleum. Slowly, she raised her gaze to meet his. "I was unmarried with a small child to take care of and—and I fell in love with him. Later, when I found out what he'd done to his first wife, I lost respect for the man. Oh, I knew about him being a gangster, but that was his business, not mine. When I found out how he treated her, though, not to mention the total disregard for his child, all I could think about was where I'd be if he got me pregnant. I could no longer live with him. I brought you down here to Mobile to live with my parents. When he didn't bother to come after us or even call, I filed for a divorce."

"I'm sorry. I didn't know."

He remembered once asking why they'd moved away from New York, and when they'd be going back. As the months passed, he'd gradually accepted that the days Vince would teach him to play cards when his mother went shopping or slip a dollar into his pocket every now and then were over.

"There's a lot I never told you. You were only twelve," she spat out.

He'd watched her face tighten, knowing her temper rose again like a roller coaster starting up another hill. He also noticed how much she had aged in the four years he'd been at college, but anger only intensified the effect.

"Don't you see, son? He'll get you up there under any pretense that works and then get his hooks into you. He'll wine and dine you and compliment you on a job well done, and then ask for some tiny favor..." She began to pace, putting some space between them before stopping and turning toward him, a finger raised. "Mark my word, Johnny, it'll appear innocent, but if you agree, you'll have sold your soul to the devil. And once you've done that little favor, you'll find yourself knee-deep in the family business."

The tirade, even the bitter accusations hurled at him about Vince, could be understood and handled, but tears were another matter. His mother seldom cried, but when she did, it ripped out his heart. She would never know how often he'd stood outside her bedroom door over the years and listened to the muffled sounds of her sobbing into a pillow.

So, when she stood there with her fists clenched at her sides and tears streaming down her face, he'd stepped forward to take her in his arms for a hug. "Mother, I'm *not* joining his business. You have nothing to worry about. My degree is in engineering-aeronautics, nothing that would benefit his organization. I'm going to design planes. Period."

Her eyes had glistened when she leaned back to look up into his face. "Never forget who Vince is—where his money comes from. Don't forget what the man does for a living. He loves you, but he lives a dangerous life. I didn't want you taking his money for college. That was your choice, but Vince doesn't do anything without expecting payment. Mark my words, he'll want something from you as repayment on his investment—"

"Here you go, buddy. Safe and sound," the taxi driver's gruff voice announced.

John popped his eyes open, momentarily confused as he slid up straighter on the seat.

New York.

In front of the Ritz.

A deep sigh slipped out. He'd hated leaving his mother on such a sour note. He understood her concern, but she needed to trust him to turn Vince down if the man asked him to work for the Giovanni family. He'd been taught in school that history tended to repeat itself, so Vince could just as easily end up like the boss before him. Dead.

He simply felt he owed his benefactor at least the opportunity to help him celebrate. That wasn't asking too much.

With her final words ringing in his ears, he rubbed his face and mentally prepared to meet his stepfather.

The cabby hopped from the car and rounded the hood, halting when a young man, impeccably dressed in the latest fashion of wide-collared suit and baggy, pleated slacks with cuffs, strode up to him. Some bills were tucked into an outstretched hand.

John stepped onto the sidewalk, then stood watching while the driver silently handed the nameless man his overnight satchel, gave a lazy salute, and then rounded the hood to slide behind the wheel of the cab. The last glimpse he had was the cabby still chomping the wad of gum as he glanced over a shoulder and then shot out into the flow of traffic.

Without knowing why, a shiver ran down his back.

"If you'll follow me, Mr. Staples, I'll take you to the gentleman waiting for you."

With a nod, he fell in behind the man until they were inside the hotel, then stepped forward to walk beside him toward the elevator.

"Congratulations on your recent graduation."

"Thank you."

John glanced over when he continued past the elevators. The concierge stepped from behind a counter, then glanced around and stepped back, his gaze dropping to study the reservation book as if it were of great importance.

This felt wrong. Vince had said they'd meet at the Ritz.

He slowed, frowning as the young man put several paces between them before glancing over his shoulder. "This way, sir."

Questions and possible consequences of a wrong decision played through his mind—weighed, but then discarded faster than a blink. Sweat beaded along his upper lip. Maybe he should have spent a little more time considering those consequences before accepting the invitation, but at this point, what choice did he have?

They exited the building through a rear door where a black sedan waited. The well-dressed young man stepped forward, opened the car door, and stood sentinel.

John hesitated for a moment, then, with heart pounding like a jack-hammer, he climbed into the back seat, the whole time praying these men worked for Vince and not the older man's enemies.

The driver kept to the back roads, but John recognized the streets and soon relaxed.

They arrived at the compound within thirty minutes. He remembered days spent playing on the high stone walls that surrounded several acres of lawns, trees, and a large house, built with thick, concrete walls overlaid with river rocks.

The arched trellis was still intact with thick-rooted vines climbing up the sides and across the top, and with huge clumps of purple flowers hanging down like bunches of grapes.

Wisteria.

Now, why in the world do I remember that?

Once standing outside the car, he surveyed the area. "Hardly anything has changed since I was last here."

The driver shrugged, then lifted an arm to point off to the right, indicating the path leading toward the backyard.

"Friendly sort," John muttered, adjusting his tie and running a hand along his shirt to assure it was tucked in properly.

He felt a presence press up near his back. A shudder ran down his spine even as he sucked in a breath and hesitated. But just as quickly, logic replaced fear. Why would anyone have anything against him? Besides, surely no one other than Vince and his men even knew about the visit.

Still, when a hand gripped his shoulder, he jerked around, prepared to face whatever threat had closed in.

Instantly, his fist relaxed. "Leo," he said, releasing

a nervous laugh as Vince's lieutenant wrapped him in a bear hug. Two arms clamped him in a beefy vice, preventing him from drawing a breath. The man's large palm pounded on his back, threatening to leave bruises as evidence of his enthusiasm.

"Hey, boy. It's been a long time."

The embrace lasted only seconds—long enough to remind him of the card games and his first puff on a cigarette—two things that would have upset his mother had she known. John sucked in much-needed air, covered his mouth to cough once, and then drew another slow, deep breath.

"You sick, kid?" A frown sent the bushy brows darting together.

"No, no, I'm fine." He chuckled, trying to reassure his stepfather's bodyguard and best friend.

"Luggage?"

He held up the satchel that contained a toothbrush, underwear, and a clean shirt. "Nope, just this."

"Then come on, boy. Vince thought it safer for you to arrive at a hotel, but safer for him if you were brought to the house. He's waiting, and he's not exactly a patient man." Leo released a barrel laugh that drew the other guard's attention.

John straightened under the pressure of the bodyguard's arm around his shoulder as the older man took possession of the satchel with his free hand.

"I'll take care of putting this in your room. You know, the old man never changed it. All the pennants still hang on the walls."

A nod apparently satisfied him, so John changed the subject. "I've been away a lot of years. How is everyone?"

Leo glanced toward the backyard. "We've lost a few members over the years. Mostly because of one family—one who deals dirty."

He knew the man referred to the family who dealt in illegal drugs but wasn't sure why that should cause a clash with the Giovanni family who dealt in betting and liquor.

"Yeah, Vince is holding off for a bit, but soon they'll understand their mistake, and some of theirs will be on the dirt side of the grass, if you know what I mean."

The slow, low-pitched chuckle sent a shiver down John's back. The man was sharing too much. "I'm not here to join Vince. I'm here for a day or so to have a meal and share old times. I'm an aeronautical engineer now—I'm going to design planes."

Leo scrunched his brows together. "Oh, sure, kid. Sure. Sorry. I thought...well, never mind what I thought." He removed his arm from John's shoulders.

At the fence, they parted ways, Leo heading along the graveled path that led to a side door while he tossed a parting comment over a shoulder. "The old man's around back. Enjoy the visit."

He hated making the man uncomfortable, but better that than have him shell out any more information about "the business"—a business he wanted *nothing* to do with.

John nodded and moved on, but a chill ran down his back. What had his stepfather said to make Leo think he'd be joining the family? Or maybe the bodyguard just assumed he'd want to join the business.

At least the slip alerted me. I'll need to be more cautious about saying anything that can be misunderstood.

Vince no doubt had reasons for this invitation, but he wasn't the only one with an agenda. This trip was for one reason and one reason only. Sure, he wanted to see his stepfather again after so many years, but mainly, he wanted to thank him for financing the college degree. Without his help, he wouldn't now be in a position to realize his life-long dream of designing airplanes. He owed Vince a lot. Loyalty—definitely—but not his life. Of course, if his mother's prediction was right, there would soon be a job offered that he'd have to turn down.

He prayed his mother was wrong.

Behind the house, a ten-foot, ivy-covered, stone fence surrounded an acre of lawn. Giant oak trees shaded the far end of the enclosure and hid a carriage house left over from horse and buggy days.

He remembered the story about Vince finding a secret tunnel while remodeling the ten by twelve structure to house a few extra beds for times when additional guards were needed. The tunnel led to the cellar in the big house, so Vince told his new wife and stepson to hide there if the compound was ever attacked. He'd assured them only the closest family members knew about the escape route, and those privileged few knew to guard the secret at the risk of their very lives.

He still got cold chills just thinking about the nightmares he'd had as a kid—nightmares where he ran for the tunnel with the hounds of hell on his heels, but the door remained just beyond his reach. He remembered several occasions when his mother came to sit with him until he fell back asleep. Had that been when her disillusionment about being married to Vince first started?

Rounding the side of the house, he took in the cluster of maple trees that had tripled in size over the years and now completely shaded the covered, flagstone veranda where green and white lounge chairs sat in groups of threes and fours. Two burly young men stood sentinel in front of an ivy-covered lattice near the patio.

He took a deep breath and continued on.

"Johnny, my boy." Vince stood, a broad smile transforming the sharp lines of the older man's face. "Come, come," he said, heading forward. He waved his hand like a policeman directing traffic through an intersection.

John hesitated for a heartbeat. He remembered Vince as standing tall with broad shoulders and a piercing look that quailed most grown men. Satan had apparently called in some markers, and time had taken a toll.

"You're looking good, son."

He blinked a couple times when his stepfather slapped him on the back and then wrapped him in a hug that felt like old times. The older man was still strong despite the rounded shoulders and hair beginning to gray at the temples.

"How are you, Vince?" he asked, returning the embrace.

"I'm not complaining." His stepfather chuckled. "Glad you could come, boy. Here…" He turned around and motioned to one of two lounge chairs separated by a small table. "Al, remember him?" Without waiting for an answer, he continued, "For lunch, he's making that lasagna you always loved, but first, I asked him to bring us a couple tall glasses of something cool to drink. You look hot. Take your tie off and relax."

As they sat, Al stepped onto the patio carrying a tray with two cut-crystal goblets filled with ice cubes and a matching pitcher of sweetened tea. The burly bodyguard had a day's growth of whiskers and a gun strapped under his arm—but he could hold his own competing against any professional chef in town. At least as far as he was concerned.

As Al filled the glasses, John removed the tie, rolled it up, and stuffed it in a pocket of his jacket folded over the arm of his chair, then reached out to take the offering.

The first sip slid down his parched throat, easing the tightness, but not his wariness. Oh sure, he was glad to see Vince, but something was different—off key— out of balance.

He downed half the tea before relaxing his arm to set the glass on the table. The cool liquid tasted good, a hint of lemon to cut the sweetness of the brew, but it settled in his stomach to churn and irritate.

Vince leaned back, wincing slightly when he turned to set his glass beside John's. "So, how's your mother doing? How's Gracie?"

The question came as a surprise, a swing out of left field. "Do you really care—or are we just making polite conversation?" He frowned, his stomach muscles knotting. Why had he reacted with such defensiveness? There was no need to be so rude. "Sorry, that was uncalled for."

"No, no. I guess it's understandable," he said, drawing in a deep breath and allowing it to escape in a long sigh. "I still care about Gracie—regardless of what happened and…"

"What actually happened?" No way could he allow such a great opening to pass without asking one of the many questions that had nagged him over the past ten years. "Life seemed good, and then I'm being moved to Mobile, and I don't hear from you until I graduate high school. And why did you offer me the chance to go to college? While I'm appreciative, it's not as if I'm really your son or anything."

His heart pounded as the seconds ticked by while the older man only stared at him. Would the great don give him a straight answer?

The silence stretched before Vince finally nodded and settled back into the lounge chair. "That was so many years ago, but I guess I owe you an explanation— at least my side of it. I'm sure you've heard your mother's side already." He flicked at a fly buzzing near his glass.

"No. She refused to speak about you when I'd ask, and wasn't happy about this visit. Just before I came, she begged me not to join your…business."

"No, no," he said, waving a hand in dismissal. "That was never my intention. You're smart, boy, but you don't have the right temperament for this line of work. So, what are your plans for the future? Where do you want to work?"

It didn't escape his notice that Vince had sidestepped his questions, but he decided not to press him—at least not at the moment. "Hughes Aircraft is at the top of my list."

"Ah, yes, Howard." He scratched his jaw, staring off toward the end of the lawn before finally speaking.

"I met him a few years ago. He owes me a favor. I'll give him a call and put in a good word for you. Your interview will be a snap."

"No!" John's muscles tightened. "I'd rather get the job on my own, if you don't mind. I was in the top five percent of my class. I won't have a problem."

Vince's eyes widened slightly, then he slowly nodded. "Okay, if that's how you want to handle it. In fact, I admire that you want to make your own way. You were always a good boy."

The older man reached for his tea glass, nodding as if affirming his own statement. This wasn't the Vince from years before. He'd seen the man quietly bulldoze someone into doing what he wanted. Would Vince keep out of the hiring process or go behind his back? He might never know for sure, but not accepting the offer kept him free from obligation.

He gradually relaxed his shoulders but didn't totally let down his guard. There were still questions to be answered, for him...and his mother. "Vince, you sidestepped my questions a bit ago about what happened between you and my mother, but I have another question—and I'd really like to know the answer to this one." He had the man's attention, and his heart rate did a little jig, but now that he had started, forward was the only direction to go. "Before I came up here, my mother mentioned your first wife got pregnant and you kicked her out. Is that true?"

"No." Vince's face tightened, his eyes narrowing to mere slits.

The flat refusal followed by silence made him wonder if his stepfather would elaborate or issue the abrupt denial and leave it at that. He had never been afraid of Vince—never had reason to—so why was he dreading the man's answer to a simple question? If only his mother had kept her concerns to herself.

He forced himself to be patient and wait. It didn't take long.

"My first wife and I were young." His scowl eased as he shifted his focus down to large, strong hands. "When I first saw Sadie, it was *un colpo di fulmine.* Love at first sight." A deep sigh slowly released into the sultry afternoon breeze. "She thought I was a business man." He smiled, a shrug barely moving his shoulders. "I wasn't sure how she'd take me being a family lieutenant, so I kept that part to myself." He heaved another big exhale and raised his gaze to again stare out across the lawn toward the grove of trees. "Maybe that was wrong. Needless to say, it caused quite a fight when she eventually found out. She was a *mulinyan,* you know, not Italian. My father told me when I turned eighteen to enjoy the girls, but when I married, be sure she was a good, Catholic girl, and above everything else, she had to be Italian. But I was in love, you know?" He chuckled softly, reaching up to press a hand over his heart.

John remained silent, waiting, not wanting to interrupt the flow.

"She finally asked, and I admitted the truth, but it frightened her. I guess I don't blame her, especially since the don, my uncle, was killed in a dispute between two of the families not six months later." He sighed, reached for the glass, and drained it. "Unfortunately for our marriage, I was the don's replacement. I had no problem with the new job, but my little Sadie turned sullen and moody. I'm knee-deep in a major counter attack—the men all going to the mattresses, you know—and one morning, I find my wife has disappeared during the night."

"Where did she go?" If Vince was being honest with him, then it didn't sound as if he'd kicked out his wife as his mother believed.

He fanned the fly away again. "I got business taken care of here and then had a couple of my men find her. She'd moved out to California."

His stepfather smiled for the first time. John could see the fondness in his expression. But if he still cared, why were they not together? "Why did you divorce her?"

The older eyes narrowed, but after a few moments, he drew in a breath and said simply, "I loved Sadie, but she never understood my way of life."

John frowned as Vince flicked his hand in a jerky wave, as if wiping the slate clean from years earlier. Was it that easy for the man to dismiss his former wife?

"I made sure she got a job and that the owner of the boarding house where she lived offered her free rent for managing the place."

"But why didn't you just go get her?" His next thought hit him in the stomach like an angry fist. Not divorcing his wife would have meant his own mother would have never married Vince—and he would have missed out on having a father, even for those few precious years. He held a breath, waiting for Vince's answer.

"Things were still volatile between the families, and it wasn't safe here. The day I found out that Sadie was expecting a baby, I did almost fly out there to haul her home, but another family don thought the time was right to come after me," he explained, tapping his own chest. "When you're young, some think that makes you inexperienced and lacking what it takes to order hits that need to happen. I had to prove myself."

John didn't bother asking what had transpired for Vince to gain the respect of the other dons. All through high school, he'd read in the newspaper about the long-term Castellammarese war going nationwide when two of their leaders were killed. Eventually, Lucky Luciano somehow got the five New York families, the Chicago Outfit, and the Buffalo Mafia to join forces to regulate the Mafia in America, but it had been a bloody business. The papers reported the American Mafia, or "La Cosa Nostra," was ruled by a group of men called "The Commission." He'd cut articles from the newspaper, especially those with Vince's name listed, and kept a scrapbook, fascinated by the organization, even while being appalled by the death and destruction.

"It took some months to straighten things out, and by then, she'd had a baby girl. I was angry at first, but my consigliere convinced me Sadie and Hannah were safer not being associated with me, and since she was using her maiden name, chances were good no one would ever suspect. For their safety, I allowed them to live in Los Angeles. Of course, if she'd had a boy, everything would have been different. A boy needs a father—someone to teach him how to be a man. But a girl..." He shrugged, raising both hands, palms up. "I sent a man to watch out for them—just to be sure they were safe, that our enemies didn't know where Sadie and the baby lived. He let me know if either of them needed anything."

Vince waved a hand in the air as if dismissing

something as unimportant. John frowned, not sure how to deal with such easy disregard of a wife and child. Sure, he didn't have either of those things himself, but he couldn't imagine living that far from a woman he loved, or not being involved in his child's life.

"Anyway, after three years, I slipped a few thousand dollars under the table and quietly had the marriage annulled."

The man's indifference to having a little girl left John shaken. Vince's delivery was cold, unemotional. Over the years, he'd learned more about the mafia, so his youthful hero-worship had dimmed, but he had always respected the man's concern for his employees and his family. Now, he wasn't sure what to say next.

After a minute, Vince stood, and John followed the older man's lead, moving into the house. "Something smells wonderful in here." He didn't stop the chuckle when his stomach added its unique comments to the conversation.

On the way to the dining room, his host stopped at the upright piano and reached for an oval-framed picture. "It's five years old, but this is my Hannah when she graduated high school."

He took the offered picture and stared down into the face of a young teen whose smile radiated with joy and excitement—excitement in life and her accomplishment as she held up a diploma.

The chill started low in his back and spread up to raise bumps on his arms. She was young, but he felt a connection that he couldn't explain. She was innocent and happy—what he wanted for himself. He couldn't remember the last time he'd smiled with abandon and actually felt jovial and carefree.

"She's very pretty, Vince," he said, handing back the picture and then wondering why he felt a momentary emptiness.

"Looks just like her mother."

His first wife must have been a very beautiful woman then. As Vince set the picture back in its prominent place, John suspected the man perhaps had never gotten over his first love.

"Come on, boy. Al has lunch ready."

The next hour was spent eating some of the best Italian food he'd ever had and talking about the fun they'd shared when he lived in the compound. All too soon, the lighthearted conversation ended, and Vince got serious. He pushed his plate out of the way and rested his elbows on the tablecloth.

"I just thought about something. You're going to work—apply to work—at Hughes Air, and you'll need a place to stay. I just happen to know about an apartment house not too far from there—a boardinghouse owned by someone I know—and I heard there's a room for rent. It's apparently pretty nice and not too far from the trolley line. I know you don't want my help with your job interview, but can I at least help you out with a call to hold the room for you?"

John hesitated. He didn't want to accept any more help that might obligate him to Vince in the future.

"Come on, my boy, let me do you this one little thing."

Surely, as long as he paid his own rent, there wouldn't be a problem. Besides, it was the least he could do to let his former stepfather and benefactor give him a helping hand. Not to mention the time it would take for him to find a place of his own. His mother never had to know that Vince helped him find a place to live.

"Sure. Just give me the address. That sounds great. Thanks."

"Good, good. You know, Hannah lives in that same boarding house."

John stopped chewing and swallowed. His chest tightened, each breath an effort, as if the words tossed out with such nonchalance had sucked all the air from the room. He fastened his gaze on the don, waiting for what he feared was coming. Had he been set up? Vince looked a bit sheepish, then frowned when John chose to remain silent.

"Well, boy, I guess you need to know the whole story." He hesitated a few more moments, then lifted his chin a bit, narrowed his eyes slightly, and started. "Recently—a few months ago—Sadie was crossing the street and got hit by a taxi. She eventually died from the injuries."

Not sure what to say in this situation, he offered the only condolence he could think of, "I'm sorry to hear that."

Vince took a deep breath, released it slowly, and continued. "I wasn't sure if it was really an accident or if someone had discovered her connection to me. If that were true, then Hannah was also in danger. Like I said before, I had someone living in one of the apartments, so I told him to do some checking. I've got enemies. If anyone finds out Hannah is my daughter and where she's living, they might use her to get to me—try to control me."

He could understand the don's dilemma, loving the people close to him and wanting to keep them safe.

Still, he couldn't respect a man who lived the gangster life, believing the end justified the means.

Vince pushed the chair back and turned to directly face him. "Look, keeping Hannah safe is the last thing I can do for Sadie, but I can't go there and do it myself without putting her in danger. She's safe for now, and it needs to stay that way, but there's a struggle for power heating up, and I need all my men here to take care of day-to-day business."

His body tensed, a shadow of foreboding dimming his pleasure at seeing his stepfather again. He was catching a glimpse of the writing on the wall. The man had maneuvered him—he could feel himself being sucked in. "So, your man is leaving Los Angeles, and you want me to move into her apartment house, right? You want me to spy on your daughter?"

The smile slipped, deepening into a scowl. "No, not spy—just watch out for her and let me know if there's ever a problem." Vince reached out to place a hand on John's arm, a smile replacing the former scowl. "Son, since you're going to be out there anyway, could you do me this one little favor?"

"Vince doesn't do anything without expecting payment. Mark my words, he'll want something from you as repayment on his investment."

A chill rippled down his arms like water down a gutter.

Mother was right.

Chapter Two

"Mr. Nolan, it's Hannah—Hannah Montgomery." She knocked again and waited patiently, allowing the elderly man time to hobble to the door. Then there would be the invitation to come in while he got the rent money and the inevitable ten or fifteen minutes to catch him up on her life over the past week before she could gracefully get away to go up to her apartment and have dinner.

The door opened a crack, then swung wide. "Hello, Sunshine."

His grin showed strong teeth yellowed from years of cigars. Smoking in the apartments was forbidden, but occasionally, she smelled the distinct odor of cigar smoke. She chose to pretend ignorance since he had difficulty getting up and down even the few stairs leading to the backyard.

"I'm here for the rent, and I'm in a bit of a hurry."

"I know, I know. A pretty girl like you must be busy all the time with beaus lining up to court you. Come on in while I get it. It's still five dollars, right?"

His shoulders stooped slightly, but there was a twinkle in his eyes that reminded her of the leprechaun stories her mother read to her when she was young. A few wisps of hair were plastered across his bald head to blend with the graying thatch curled around the tops of his ears. Although not related, he was the only grandfather she'd ever known.

"Yes siree, I bet you lead them a merry chase." His shoulders jiggled as his chuckle ended on a wheezing cough.

She reached out to help steady him, but he waved away her extended hand.

Clearing his throat, Mr. Nolan slowly sucked in another breath. "Getting old is for the birds," he lamented, wagging his head from side to side as he sighed. Then he stabbed the air with a gnarled finger as he sent her a wink. "In my hay days, I'd have given those young whelps a run for their money. I can't believe you don't have a serious beau." His humph was loud, followed by mumbling about young men not knowing how to treat a lady.

Hannah's heart warmed toward the older man. He'd asked the same question every week for the past few years, showing the same concern for her single status.

"Now, you know I'm too busy right now to add anything else to my life." She followed him as he limped toward the sofa. "How have you been?"

Each morning, he sat out in front of the building, waving to the neighbors leaving for work while he kibitzed with Mr. Brannon from apartment 1-C. The two old gentlemen had known each other longer than she'd been alive and still found things to talk about. She smiled, shaking her head at the thought. Of course, maybe they said the same things each day and neither of them remembered…or cared.

"Me? Oh, I'm doing just like the weather—fair," he answered. "You know, it just ain't right for a young thing like you to be all alone. Why, I'd be courting you myself if I was forty…well, maybe fifty years younger." His eyes twinkled as a mischievous grin lifted his lips into a smile. "Of course, back in my day, I would have had to pick you up in a buggy since we didn't have cars, but that just made courtin' a bit more interesting."

"Is that how you courted Mrs. Nolan?" She wanted to kick herself for encouraging him to talk when she needed to finish and get the rent money ready to deposit in the bank.

"Yes siree bob. I'd bring along a blanket to tuck around her legs, and then we'd ride out into the countryside for a picnic after church on Sundays." He stared off over her shoulder, obviously revisiting old memories.

"Mr. Nolan, you're a cutie pie, and I love you bunches. You know that, right?"

"Yep." He chuckled, wheezing a bit as he turned, braced both hands on the arms of the upholstered chair, bent at the waist, and then dropped the last few inches onto the seat. "And I don't blame you one little bit. I'm a lovable fella," he added, laughing at his own joke. "So, how is this old world treating you?"

"I'll have you know I got to do Claudette Colbert's hair this morning. Her regular hair and make-up girl was sick, so I got to fill in." She trembled with remembered excitement at being told to work on one of her favorite actresses. Of course, she'd been the only one available, but that didn't stop her from basking in the memory of being instructed to fill in.

"And I bet she liked you—even better than her regular girl, right?" He pointed an arthritic finger toward her as he voiced his opinion.

"Well, she didn't say that, but she gave me a compliment, right in front of the head of makeup, so I guess that's good." Hannah hugged the thought close.

"It sure is. You just wait and see. One of these days, you're going to be the one in charge of make-up over there at Paramount. Mark my words." He nodded his head, affirming his prediction.

She hoped so. That would be not only a dream come true, but an answer to prayers for a pay raise. But for now, she was just thankful for having a job since her mother's income was no longer there to help make ends meet. She fought the sudden tears. Several months since her passing and she still missed her mother—her closest friend—as much as ever.

"You still dating that skinny fella?"

Hanna laughed, relaxing for the first time that day. The prior month, she'd been leaving on a date with Tom Lucio when Mr. Nolan had stepped out of his apartment. After a quick introduction, the older man said Tommy was too street smart for her, and she needed to keep looking around. He'd repeated his opinion every chance he got.

"As a matter of fact, no. He moved back to New York a couple of days ago."

"Well, Sunshine, with the cat away, the little mouse should play," he teased, winking. "Find yourself a new beau and have a little fun. All you do is work down at Paramount and then come home and work collecting rent, getting things fixed around here, and shopping for all us old folks. You need to go out and kick up your heels a little before you get too old."

It wasn't the first time he'd told her to find someone new, but she still laughed at the indignant snort he always tacked onto the end of his lecture. "I'm twenty-three. I have lots of years to 'kick up my heels,' " she told him, leaning over to give him a quick hug, then smiled at the red tinge flushing his face and ears. "I'd love to stay and talk with you, but I gotta get going."

"Okay, little one. The money's on the counter over there." He pointed toward the kitchen. "Now, don't be so long before you drop in again. It's always good talking with you."

"Okay, Mr. Nolan. I'll see you next week." She waved, but her mind was already refocused on the issue that had cost her sleep the past few nights. Money, always in short supply. The fear of it haunted her evening hours.

I'd soon be living on the street if I didn't get free rent for being the manager.

Her feet ached as she climbed the stairs. All she could think about was getting her shoes off, warming up the leftover macaroni and cheese, and then calling it a night. Tomorrow would be another long day at work, and she'd agreed to go by the grocers for Mrs. Wilson in 1-D. *Poor lady can hardly walk any longer, let alone carry a bag of goods up the front steps.*

Once in her apartment, she sagged back against the cool wood. "Mother, what were you thinking about when you stepped out in front of that taxi?" Tears still came easily, and she swiped at both cheeks before pushing away from the door to stand in front of the end table where a gold-framed picture was prominently displayed. "Mama," she whispered, "I miss you so much." She ran a finger down the glass, tracing along the familiar face.

Her eyes drifted closed as she slowly drew a deep breath, taking in the fading fragrance of her mother's favorite perfume dabbed sparingly behind each ear just to take something of the beloved woman with her through the day. The fragrance brought with it the comforting memories of unconditional love and security.

With a deep breath, she sobered, blinking her eyes several times. Of course, memories of unconditional love would always remain, but security was now a bit elusive.

Action fixes what worrying won't.

"You're right, Mother," she murmured, wiping away a lone tear. "Feeling sorry for myself isn't going to put food on the table." Everyone had told her that time would ease the pain—the loss. Obviously, it would take more than a few months.

She hesitated long enough to glance around the room that once held so much joy—and now only memories.

Hannah dropped her purse and the collected rent on the dinette table, then sank down to slip off her shoes. She glanced again at the picture of her mother and herself, taken a few years earlier at her high school graduation—so young, facing the future head-on, and beaming at the camera.

Despite a heart that still ached at the loss, the deep-seated love they had shared brought a tender smile to her face. Her mother had been a wise, honest woman.

"Thanks, Mama," she whispered. "I intend to follow in your footsteps—wherever they take me."

She picked up her discarded shoes and headed for the bedroom closet. After placing the low-heeled pumps on the shelf, she stood staring at her meager wardrobe. Her mother had always loved nice clothes, opting for one classic, tailored outfit over two or three less expensive ones.

"Quality is always in style."

Hannah closed the closet door and wandered into her mother's room, running a finger along the dresser and vowing to dust everything before going to bed. Beside the almost-empty bottle of perfume sat a small oval frame of her maternal grandparents. Neither smiled. Instead, they both stood straight and sober as soldiers in front of a clapboard house with one window and front steps that sagged to the right. Sad.

Hannah often wondered why there was no picture of her father. Not even a wedding picture. Had they thought there would be plenty of time, but instead, he'd been killed?

It did no good to ask questions she could never answer.

She turned to stare around the room. *Everything has a place, and everything should be in its place.* The sigh slipped out. That adage had been one of her mother's strictest rules. Tidiness was second-nature now.

Hannah hesitated near the bed where her mother's slippers still peeked out from under the dust ruffle but didn't stop until she stood in front of the closet door. After only a moment's hesitation, she grasped the clear-glass knob and opened the cupboard, closing her eyes to breath in the smell of wool and musky perfume that still lingered in the small, closed-up space.

The essence of Sadie Montgomery.

When she opened her eyes, the dresses hung in

precise order, like good soldiers awaiting orders to serve. She reached up, tenderly running her fingertips across the smooth material of a tailored white suit edged with navy piping. A spot of light overshadowed by shades of gray, brown, and black, but each dress a favorite despite most being cast-offs from leading starlets when they'd grown tired of the garment. When offered, her mother had accepted them with gratitude and excitement.

Hannah smiled, relaxing her tense jaw as the memories gently washed over. Her mother had been full of contradictions. She had loved to laugh, but cried at night behind the closed door, was passionate about women's rights and temperance, but refused requests to speak at public meetings on behalf of her beliefs.

"Have you really been gone almost four months?" Her vision blurred, the tears escaping from behind closed eyes. She slowly allowed her head to bow under the weight of her loss.

The sadness gradually passed, bringing her back to the white-on-white room as she stood staring at the contents of the closet. "It's silly to leave such nice clothes to gather dust and risk being ruined by moths."

The decision was made quickly, with little agonizing. She had borrowed the dresses when her mother was alive, so the practical thing to do was move them to her closet so they'd be available for use.

She slid the dozen or so hangers together on the pole, lifted them off, and carried them to her room down the hall. A couple minutes later, she had them rearranged by color into two sections—casual and the few more formal suits. Her favorite was still the slinky, midnight-blue evening dress her mother had been given. They had both tried it on, *oohing* and *ahhing* over its slenderizing lines and naughty plunging neckline, but neither of them had ever had an occasion to wear it out for an evening.

There was satisfaction in seeing so many outfits to choose from, but the elation was short-lived. Guilt reared its ugly head. What was she thinking?

Hannah, don't be ridiculous. She immediately squashed the negative thoughts. "This is what mother would want," she whispered into the tomb-like silence of the room. She then slid some of the outfits forward so she could put her mother's calf-length wool coat at the back.

That's when she noticed a seam was separating on the pocket.

With reverent care, she took the hanger from the pole, lifted the sewing box from the shelf that also held her two hats, and carried the bundle to the kitchen to repair the coat while her supper warmed.

She started by checking each pocket. In one was a trolley token, and the other held a couple folded pieces of paper. Her first inclination was to set them aside, but curiosity overruled, and she unfolded one, surprised to see bold, masculine handwriting.

Dearest Sadie,

I must return home, but the thought leaves me empty and my heart already misses you. Please tell me you're seriously considering my proposal. I want to make you happy for the rest of your life.

The note was signed with an equally bold check mark…or perhaps a "V"?

"That's strange." It was obviously written by someone who loved her mother, but her father's name

33

was Robert, and the note was definitely not signed with an "R." She puzzled over the note while she unfolded the second one.

My Dearest Sadie,

Your agreement to marry me has made me the happiest man on earth. I'll be down to get you this Friday. Be ready and we'll go to the Justice of the Peace and take care of business.

This one was signed the same way.

Hannah chuckled. "Does he think it's romantic to refer to getting married as 'taking care of business?' " Well, since she didn't marry again, it must have been written by her father, but that didn't sound like the considerate, loving man her mother described.

At least now she had something belonging to her deceased father. She clutched the notes to her chest and closed her eyes, cherishing the moment—an interrupted moment when her belly growled.

"Okay. Okay." She patted her midsection

Hannah put the macaroni and cheese on low to warm, then mended the coat and rehung it in the closet. She put the sewing box back on the shelf and slipped the notes into her treasure box.

After supper was usually spent listening to the news on the radio, but she didn't bother to turn it on. Despite the war being over and American soldiers being back home from France, most of the news reports were still depressing.

With the living-room light turned off, the furniture slowly became recognizable silhouettes. Was this what life would be like now that her last relative had died? With the loss of her mother, the future was hazy—out-of-focus, dark, and scary. Would the darkness gradually fade and allow her to see life again as she'd once hoped it would be?

Or will I always be alone?

Chapter Three

"I'll have you at the boardinghouse in nothing flat. Just relax, and I'll point out some of the city's more interesting sites along the way."

John leaned his head back, closed his eyes, and blocked out the driver's running monologue. His mind was in turmoil. The new job at Hughes would begin in two days and nothing—not his mother, Vince, or anyone else—was going to be a distraction. This was his big opportunity. Now, if only he knew whether or not he'd gotten the job on his own merits and not after a call from Vince, things would be perfect. He'd probably never know for sure.

The thought of Vince lying to him brought back memories of Sister Mary Margaret at school. The nuns had been very strict about cheating and lying—not only because bearing false witness was a sin, but to the good sister, lying was a personal pet peeve.

It still chafed that his stepfather's mob connection had been kept from him for so many years. Even after figuring out the truth, his mother had tried to deny it. That had been the one and only time he'd screamed back at her. He still cringed at the memory of calling her a liar right before slamming out of the house and riding his bike down to the river where he slung rocks into the water until his arm ached.

From that day until he graduated high school, his

mother had never mentioned Vince to him again. The way he saw it, she had kept secrets, just like Vince said he'd done with his first wife before they were married.

Lies on top of lies.

He firmed his lips into a straight line while his breaths became shallow and closer together. Lies made life a holy mess when the truth finally came to light.

John shoved a hand through his hair. It rankled that he'd be committing Sister Mary Margaret's unpardonable sin by hiding the truth from Vince's daughter. Even if he didn't outright lie to her, he'd be holding back facts and going behind her back to keep her father informed. His frown deepened as he made his decision, instant and final. He would tell the don nothing unless a problem arose that he couldn't handle himself. Period.

How *had* Vince gotten him to agree to do this—especially after his mother warned him? She'd said it would start with a seemingly innocent, little favor that appeared harmless, and then the big man would set the hook. He should have listened to her and turned down his stepfather's invitation for a celebration in New York. When he returned home to Alabama, he didn't tell her about being trapped into helping Vince. He even waited two days before mentioning he'd acquired an apartment.

His teeth clenched as he shook his head. More lies.

He squared his shoulders, finished accepting things from Vince. The round-trip airplane ticket to New York had been a graduation gift, but thankfully, he'd sold enough text books to underclassmen to afford the ticket to California, with some money left over for a rainy day.

Vince and mother would never do anything to intentionally hurt me, but they're a couple thousand miles away. From now on, I'll make my own decisions and pay my own way.

Still, thoughts of Vince brought Hannah Giovanni—or rather, Montgomery—to mind. What would she be like?

"Here we are, sir."

The taxi driver pulled to the curb and hopped out, heading to the trunk to unload the two cases while John stepped out onto the sidewalk and stared up at the row of buildings lining the street.

The Hannigan Boardinghouse, no doubt a formerly handsome building, now carried the gray hair and wrinkles of an aged classic. Crammed between two identical buildings, a wooden sign, faded from years of intense Southern California sun, hung over the door to distinguish it from its neighbors.

Down the street, a corner market boasted its presence with a small neon sign that some might think gaudy, while others would think progressive. Functional. That's how he saw it.

"I think you'll like living here," the driver continued as if no time had passed since his last comment. "Lots of famous Hollywood stars lived at Hannigan's in their beginning years—you know, before they made it big." He set the mismatched cardboard cases on the sidewalk and then turned his full attention on him, lifting his lips into a wide smile as he pocketed the fare and generous tip. "Thank you, sir, and good luck."

John nodded and turned away. After the long flight from Alabama, the relative silence surrounding him now was a welcome reprieve from the driver's endless chatter. With a leather satchel over his shoulder and a suitcase in each hand, he hesitated for another glance at the boardinghouse, wondering what tales the two-story building would tell if it could speak.

Maybe some things are better left untold.

"Oh my goodness."

The words, simple and not spoken with much volume, held a degree of exasperation.

He slid his gaze toward a young woman standing a short distance away, her eyes closed, chest heaving, and her feet apparently rooted to the spot. While he watched, a deep sigh slipped out as she opened her eyes then stooped to grab at the food scattered at her feet.

An orange scooted along the sidewalk, bouncing slightly as it tripped over a crack to roll to a stop against his shoe. He glanced down, then refocused on the slender girl wearing a flowered dress and low-heeled shoes as she slowly straightened, a tomato in each hand. Dry spaghetti noodles still lay scattered on the sidewalk. Furrowed brows scrunched over stormy eyes told how she felt about the ripped bag and her food landing on the cement.

Aching muscles from cramped airplane seating were forgotten as he watched dark hair swing forward to shield her face when she squatted again to corral more vegetables. Without taking time to analyze the increased thumping inside his chest, he set down his luggage and reached for the orange before closing the distance between them. Not waiting for permission to help, he knelt on one knee and began to gather the sticks of dried pasta. She rose and took a step back, drawing his gaze up to meet hers.

Un colpo di Fulmine.

As the thought struck, actual words stuck in a suddenly-dry throat. He swallowed once, then again. Without breaking eye contact, he slowly rose, holding the spaghetti in one hand like a bunch of flowers. Now what?

Something about the whole scene drew out a soft chuckle. "Um, sorry." He leaned to pick up the ripped bag and wrapped it around the noodles then glanced toward the boardinghouse before reconnecting with her gaze. "I'm here to see Hannah Montgomery."

Her smile gradually appeared and eventually reached her eyes. "I'm Hannah."

Gentle, soft. His stomach tightened. "You're not what I expected." Had he really voiced that thought?

She arched an eyebrow, her lips quirking to one side. The silence stretched. He'd seen her picture, but she was no longer the skinny kid in the five-year-old photo.

"I thought you were—older."

"Have I met you before?"

"No." He mentally chided himself for being careless. She must never know why he'd been sent. "I called about the room. You sounded…more mature, um, I mean…older."

Her laughter drifted toward him on the gentle afternoon breeze. His heart stuttered and dropped a beat before resuming its normal rhythm.

"Then you must be John. Nice to meet you." She shifted the second tomato into her left hand and reached out to shake.

Her skin was soft, like kitten fur, but her grip was firm. The smile remained, though her gaze shifted to take in every feature, as if sizing him up. He'd seen an analyzing look before and only hoped he passed the test.

"Thank you, ma'am."

She laughed out loud now. "Please, just call me Hannah. 'Ma'am' makes me feel—well, like the woman you apparently expected to meet."

"Okay." He lifted the bag. "Sorry about your food."

"Thankfully, it *is* mine."

When he only stared, confused, but not wanting to possibly embarrass her by asking her to clarify, she flushed a becoming pink and quickly continued.

"I shop for a few of the elderly tenants who have a difficult time getting down the steps and walking. I'm just glad it wasn't for one of them."

"Oh, I see. Well, let me get my bags and maybe you can show me to my apartment?"

"Sure."

With the orange stuffed in his suit pocket and the spaghetti bag in the other, he slung the satchel strap higher on his shoulder. After hoisting the two suitcases, he followed her up the steps into the boardinghouse and then on up to the second floor. He kept his gaze trained on her ankles, noting her small, low-heeled black shoes while he fought to avoid lifting his focus to her backside that swayed slightly in his line of vision.

"Let me drop this food in my apartment and get a key for you. I'll be right out."

He set down the suitcases and reached into his pockets to retrieve her spaghetti and orange. With the items now safely in her hands, he leaned against the wall to wait.

What have I gotten myself into?

Sure, he had to live somewhere, but he planned to stick to his decision not to report to Vince about his daughter. He was still shaking his head when Hannah stepped out into the hall.

She stopped a few inches away, frowning slightly. "Is something wrong?"

"Oh, no." He could feel his neck flushing at being caught. "I was just thinking about…something."

Hannah nodded, her lips tipping up into a smile that almost instantly disappeared before she moved past him to cross the hall and unlock the door to another apartment. He glanced toward the ceiling and asked for divine help in not doing anything else to make himself look more stupid.

With a discreet distance between them, he followed her into the room. Considering the building's obvious age, the apartment was a pleasant surprise. He set the suitcases down and surveyed the over-sized living room with its large window that looked down on the street below. The narrow kitchenette to his left had a black and white, square-tiled floor and black tile accents against the antique-white painted walls. The narrow, four-burner stove/oven and small refrigerator looked almost new, as did the white tablecloth covering the small dinette table.

Impressive.

"The bedroom is that way." She pointed but remained standing near the door as she stretched out a hand to give him the key. "If you need anything at all, please don't hesitate to come over or leave a note under my door." She stepped out into the hallway, but hesitated and turned back. "I work during the day, but

I'm home by six most evenings."

"Thanks. I'm sure everything will be fine. Have a good evening. Oh," he added, stopping her exit, "is there a coffee house or restaurant near here so I can get a little supper? I haven't been to the store for groceries yet." He shrugged, giving her a sheepish grin.

"I'm sorry. How rude of me not to think of that." She hesitated, then continued, "I'm going to make spaghetti. It's nothing fancy, but if you'd like to come over in about half an hour, you can join me. I'm not the best cook, but it's passable."

John hesitated, mentally vacillating between not wanting to impose and wanting the opportunity to get to know this woman better. How else could he convince himself that the first reaction to her—the feeling of having his legs knocked out from under him—had been just a fluke?

"That would be very kind. I'll be over later. Thanks."

She nodded, linked her fingers, then cleared her throat and relaxed both arms to her sides before nodding again and quickly backing from the room. She raised a hand to wave, then smiled quickly and reached out to pull the door closed between them.

John stood in the middle of the room, staring at the door. Had he really made her that nervous? He smiled, then chuckled, and then laughed out loud. Had she also felt *something* when they'd met?

"Good." He didn't really have time for a relationship right now, but she'd been cute when she got all flustered and beat a hasty retreat.

John tried to put Hannah out of his mind over the next half-hour, but the very thought of seeing her again and sitting down across from her for dinner had his heart rate elevated. He forced himself to concentrate on hanging his clothes in the closet and putting his toiletries in the tiny bathroom off his bedroom. Unfortunately, he was finished within fifteen minutes, leaving too much time to analyze why he felt excited yet a little apprehensive about spending the evening with such a beautiful woman.

Vince's daughter.

The thought grabbed his stomach and twisted it into a knot. Like a flag flapping in the breeze and suddenly going limp, he sobered, imagining Vince's reaction if he knew what was going through his stepson's mind.

Dinner—just a polite, neighborly gesture. Right?

By the time he knocked on Hannah's apartment door, John had considered several ways Vince might react if he found out his stepson was having dinner with his daughter, and the consequences of each scenario. In the don's world, men had probably disappeared permanently for less.

The thought made him shudder.

The door opening swept away thoughts of Vince and focused all of them on Hannah.

A lovely name for a lovely woman.

She still wore the flowered dress, but she now had on crocheted slippers, much like his mother wore at home. The shoulder-length, dark hair hung in soft waves that swung toward her face when she turned her head and moved back to allow him to enter.

"Hi, come on in."

"It smells good in here. What can I do to help?"

"Everything is ready. If you'd like to take a seat at

the table, I'll dish up the food."

He nodded, wishing she'd keep talking. The soft-spoken words made his taunt stomach muscles relax—an effect that brought back long-forgotten memories. It wasn't the words, but the soothing tone, like his mother's voice in the middle of the night when he'd been a child and sick. He frowned slightly, shaking his head as if erasing the thoughts. Maybe he shouldn't have come.

"I'd like to thank you for coming to dinner tonight." She sat a bowl of spaghetti on the table before she lowered her gaze and turned away to get a salad and bowl of dressing from the refrigerator. "Sorry," she said, laughing gently as her gaze darted from the food to meet his stare and then away. "I just hate eating alone, and since my mother passed a few months ago, I haven't had anyone... Anyway, thanks for taking pity on me," she ended with a soft smile while lifting the pitcher to fill their glasses with water.

"Who's taking pity here?" He chuckled, hoping to ease the tension, but unable to check the sudden sympathy for the obviously lonely woman. "I was expecting to sit in a restaurant alone since I haven't shopped for food yet. Of course," he added with a shrug, "I can't cook a decent meal even if I have food. I think it's sweet that you took pity on *me*." Man, he loved it when she laughed.

"Okay then, we'll call it even." She lowered onto the chair and spread a cloth napkin on her lap before closing her eyes and bowing her head.

Silence continued for several seconds before he realized she expected him to ask a blessing on the meal. He hadn't prayed since leaving Catholic school. Well, maybe a few times, but certainly not out loud—or in public.

His heart pounded, and sweat warmed his forehead. "Lord, please bless this food which we are about to receive and use it to nurture our bodies. Amen."

Hannah moved her hand in a cross over her chest before she opened her eyes and glanced at him. "Thank you." She smiled and reached to pass him the spaghetti.

The only noise in the room for the next fifteen minutes was utensils scraping against plates as they ate. He frowned, his mind whirling on a possible reason— other than just having met—for being uncomfortable around each other. Had she really wanted to invite him to dinner, or had she just felt obligated?

Only one way to find out.

She looked up from her plate when he cleared his throat. "You know, if we don't talk, we might as well both be eating alone in our own apartments."

She stared at him—as if his stating the obvious had taken her by surprise. Her eyes twinkled in the soft light of the lamp at her back. Then she smiled—an innocent widening of her lips that transformed her from attractive to stunning.

"You're beautiful." Without thinking first, he'd spoken the words, not as an endearment, but merely an observation, but he instantly knew he owed her an apology. Her neck and cheeks flushed pink, and she lowered her gaze to the table. He'd overstepped. "I'm sorry. I didn't mean to embarrass you or make you feel uncomfortable."

"No, it's fine, and you're right about the lack of conversation. So, tell me about yourself and what you're doing here in Los Angeles."

He hesitated a moment to swallow and then began. "I'm from Mobile, Alabama, where my mother still lives, and I recently graduated college with an engineering degree, specializing in aircraft design. I just got a job at Hughes Aircraft." He took a sip of water and looked at her again. "How about you? Have you always lived in California?" It would be interesting to see how much her mother had told her about Vince.

"Yes. In fact, I've always lived right here in this boardinghouse, or at least as long as I can remember, anyway. My mother worked at Paramount doing hair and make-up for the movie stars. I wanted to learn the trade, so she taught me all she knew, and then I went to beauty school. Now, I work in her old job at the movie studio."

"Tell me about your mother." He leaned his head to the side, indicating the picture he'd noticed on his arrival. "She's very beautiful."

"Thank you. Yes, she was." She blinked rapidly several times, then swallowed before trying to speak again. "There were good times and bad, but regardless of what else was happening, she loved to laugh and have fun."

"You look like her." He smiled, glancing from the photo to stare at her before his smile widened. "Beautiful."

A soft laugh slipped out. "Thank you, but I must have my father's eyes, and when mother and I were out in the sun for a day, she'd burn and I'd tan."

"Interesting." She didn't appear to know about her Italian heritage—and he couldn't tell her. "You don't know your father?"

"No, he died when I was young. When my parents

met, he was a few years older and already in law enforcement."

John covered his surprise with a cough, unsure how to react to the factitious father her mother had created—one who was a complete opposite from reality.

Hannah frowned slightly. "Are you okay?"

"Yeah, great—just great," he mumbled, taking another swallow of water. "How did your father die?"

"A man grabbed a little girl. There was a hostage standoff. During the final shoot-out, he was shot and killed. He died a hero. Mama said he was an honorable, loving man who put himself in the line of fire and eventually sacrificed himself to save someone else."

Devil and angel warred for control—one tempted him to press further to discover anything else she'd been told about this imaginary father, while the other told him to leave the subject alone.

The devil won. "Life isn't always what we think."

Blue eyes widened, darkening like the sky on a stormy night. "What do you mean?"

"I mean, your mother was telling you about her husband who was…well, not in the picture any more. It's natural to remember only the good things."

Her gaze narrowed as she digested his statement and probably wondered what he was trying to say. He wondered himself.

John stood. "That was delicious. Can I help you clear the table?"

"No, just relax." She stared as if wanting to ask a question, but instead, blinked several times and stood to gather the two plates, glasses, and flatware. After the barest hesitation, she turned toward the kitchen.

Restless, he wandered about the room, picking

things up and then putting them down. With hands now shoved into his pockets, he fought the inner struggle. Tell her or keep his mouth shut? The decision was not difficult. Each time she spoke about her father, pride radiated out like the sun shining on a summer day. No. He couldn't burst her bubble. He sat on the sofa to wait for her. Besides, he *had* promised Vince.

"So, do you have any other relatives around here?" He felt sleazy for asking a question he already knew the answer to, but how else could he keep his cover intact?

"No. Both my parents were only children, and their parents have both passed. My father's father died over in France in the last war."

John remained silent. So, her mother had made up a father who, interestingly enough, was the total opposite of Vince. He couldn't admit to knowing more about her father than she did. That wouldn't go over well at all. To start with, she wouldn't believe him. The minute he mentioned Vince and the New York crime families, she'd probably think he was one of them and evict him.

"I'm sorry for all your losses."

She shrugged. "I never knew my father, but what's worse, I don't even have a picture. I don't know if I resemble him or just my mother. Everyone said mother and I looked enough alike to be sisters, but do I have his ears? Or his smile?"

The pause lengthened until he squirmed. If only there was another subject, but his mind was blank. "I wish I could have met your mother." Already the deceit gnawed at his stomach, not allowing the spicy Italian food to settle. Regardless, he had to ask the next question. "How old was she when she passed? She must have been awfully young."

"Forty-two." The silence hung before she sucked in a deep breath and continued, "She was coming home from the store, and a taxi hit her when she crossed a street." Leaving the dishes to soak in the sink, she returned to the living room and sat down on the opposite end of the sofa.

"Did the police check it out?"

"Why? It was just an accident—the taxi came around the corner, and there she was. Or at least that's what the driver told the police." She cleared her throat before continuing, "I don't think he was even arrested." Hannah glanced down and ran her finger along the outer edge of a flower on her skirt, tracing the pattern and making a slight crease with her fingernail.

"Again, I'm sorry for your loss." He reached across the short distance, laid a hand on her wrist, and waited for her to lift her gaze. "Really, I know it's tough losing a parent. My father died when I was about five. My life changed forever, but then, after two or three years, my mother married another guy. He helped fill the void…at least a little bit and for a short while."

"They didn't stay together?"

"No, only a few years."

"My mother never married again—although there's a slight chance she had a gentleman friend after my father died, one I never knew about. I found a couple of notes in the pocket of her winter coat. I've wondered if they were from a man she worked with, or maybe even the man who owns the boardinghouse."

"The boardinghouse owner?"

"Mmm-hmm. He paid for mother's funeral. Or maybe he was just being nice since she'd lived here so long and worked for him so many years. Anyway, did you stay in touch with your stepfather?"

John hesitated. At least this was a question not requiring a lie. "Not over the years, but then I graduated high school, and out of the blue, he called and offered to pay for me to go to college."

Her face brightened into a huge smile. "Really? How wonderful for you. I received a small stipend that paid for school, but I also had to take a job waiting tables at the local coffee house to pay for all the supplies I needed to get my license to do hair and makeup. Your stepfather must be a wonderful guy."

The thought of her working her way through school while her own father paid *his* way strengthened his resolve to confront Vince at his first opportunity. How could the man have not paid for every bit of Hannah's education as well? If her father cared about her enough to want her safe, why didn't he find a way to pay for her school? Anger began to build. How should he respond to her statement?

After a hesitation, he offered a tight smile and shrugged. "He has his moments, I guess."

He might think I owe him something in payment for the education, but he owes me *something as well. I want an explanation for this.*

He clenched the hand resting in his lap into a fist. Maybe not soon, but some day, one way or the other, he'd get that answer.

Chapter Four

The trolley conductor clanged a warning at each street crossing and before every stop to pick up or drop off passengers. John sat with his tie loosened, his head leaning against the window frame, and eyes closed. Various conversations were taking place around him, but he chose to block out the noise. Mentally and physically tired, he tried to clear out all conscious thoughts, but his subconscious refused to cooperate. Instead, his thoughts preferred to focus on the first day at Hughes Aircraft Company. He hadn't known what to expect, but it certainly hadn't been the roller-coaster ride of thrills he received.

He'd expected to be shown to a drafting table, but instead, after being introduced to his supervisor, they'd walked out to the hanger area to see the plane currently being built. The whole concept of being involved in the creation of airplanes was exciting enough to have him floating on a cloud. Then a workman turned around, and he was suddenly standing face-to-face with the pilot who, only a year earlier, had broken the record for flying a plane over land.

Howard Hughes.

The man gave him a tight smile and stretched out a hand. Unable to think what to say to a man he'd idolized for several years, John had simply shaken hands and nodded. This would have been enough, but then Mr. Hughes motioned for him to step up and check out the wing design of the plane and offer suggestions. He still couldn't believe how tongue-tied he'd been at first, but, thankfully, he'd soon relaxed. One of the great minds of aviation design had actually discussed not only the wing design, but the retractable wheel mechanism with him.

Wonders never cease.

The cherry on top of his first-day sundae had been discussing future plans with him. He'd never forget the conversation.

"So, John, I'm considering making a transcontinental flight in the next year or so. Burbank, California to Newark, New Jersey—in less than seven and a half hours. Do you think it's possible?"

He couldn't believe the man had asked his opinion, but words seemed to just pop out of his mouth. *"Sir, I'm not sure, but I'm convinced that if anyone can do it, you have a better than average chance of succeeding."*

Looking back on the conversation now, he couldn't decide if his response had sounded awestruck or like he was trying to tell the man what he wanted to hear in order to get ahead in the company. The very thought Mr. Hughes might think the latter made his stomach cramp.

Still, just thinking about the brilliant man's future plans to make a record-breaking, trans-American flight gave him chills. His new boss had vision and drive like no one he'd ever met before.

And now I work in the man's sphere. I get to help in reaching his goals.

John stood when the trolley was a block from the boardinghouse. By the time it stopped, he had maneuvered himself around the people standing in the aisle and was able to step down onto the sidewalk.

"Hey, young man."

He smiled at the elderly gentleman sitting in a chair on the small porch of the boardinghouse. Could this be one of the older folks Hannah bought groceries for? He smiled and lifted a hand in greeting.

"Yes siree, saw you from my window this morning," he said, hitching his thumb over his right shoulder, indicating the first-floor apartment. "Looks like you got yourself an important job, what with that suit and briefcase. Lawyer?"

John chuckled, coming to a stop at the top of the steps near the wicker chair. "No. I design airplanes. I work over at Hughes Aircraft." He felt a swelling of pride just saying it out loud.

"Now look at you. Ain't that something? Flying up there like a bird." A finger knobby with arthritis pointed upward. "This old Earth must be a sight to behold from way up there." He shook his head and chuckled, reaching out a hand to shake. "Name's Nolan—Caleb Nolan."

"Nice to meet you, sir. I'm John Staples." They shook hands, and he prepared to say good-bye and leave until the man spoke again.

"From the South, are you? I can hear it in your voice." Old eyes squinted against the brilliant setting sun.

"Yes, sir. Mobile, Alabama."

"Ay, I knew I could hear that southern drawl. I can spot 'em every time. Well, don't let me keep you. Just wanted to say howdy and welcome."

"Thank you, sir." He took a step toward the screen

door but stopped when Mr. Nolan spoke again.

"What do you think of our landlady?"

"Hannah?" The older man watched him with an intent stare, but only nodded. "Um, fine, I guess. She's very polite, and…"

"And pretty as a picture." Mr. Nolan wheezed a bit when he laughed at answering his own question. "Well, I already like you better than that last one who lived upstairs before you. He was sniffing around her skirt. I see things. I know." He nodded his head with importance. "And then there's that little pip-squeak she's dated a couple of times after her mama passed. Trouble. Nothing but trouble. Mark my words, he ain't worth a plug nickel."

For reasons he couldn't explain, John's ears perked up, and suspicions began to form. The man who vacated the apartment probably worked for Vince, but who was the other one? "You said she's dating him? It's not like he's bothering her with unwanted attention, right?"

"Naw, nothing like that. Lest ways, I don't believe so. It's just that he looks to be the lazy sort. Hangs around and always finds an excuse to touch her. You know, holds her hand, or touches her arm. He's also big on putting his arm around her shoulders or her waist. It's not right." He made a tsking noise several times while shaking his head. "Maybe you can talk some sense into her."

"Me?" His mind jerked back from pondering if the man hanging around was a threat to realizing the old gentleman had a gleam in his eye and was encouraging him to get to know their landlady a bit better.

No, he didn't need interruptions right now, despite

how good a cook she was or how pretty she looked with her hair pulled back and tucked up under the wide-brimmed hat she'd worn earlier today when leaving for work. Mr. Nolan wasn't the only one who put his street-view window to good use.

"We just met. I doubt she'd put much faith in anything I said, and besides, I don't know anything about the man."

"Well, I don't know anything for sure, but his eyes are shifty. Don't trust a man with shifty eyes," he concluded, tapping his black cane down on the porch.

He smiled when the older gentleman's lips quirked down at one corner, as if the very thought of the man gave him a sour stomach. He wasn't sure what to say about the guy he'd never seen. *The less the better.* "Mr. Nolan, it's been a pleasure meeting you." He chuckled softly when the pruned lips immediately tilted up.

"Same to you, young man. Now, you be good to our girl and treat her right, you hear?"

John opened his mouth to remind him he and Hannah weren't dating each other, but the old man was already waving at an elderly woman, calling out to her as she hobbled down the sidewalk.

"Hi, Millie. How're you doing today?"

John shook his head, chuckled again, and entered the boardinghouse. The self-appointed Cupid had them linked, regardless of anything he might say to the contrary. The likelihood of changing the man's mind was probably nil-to-nothing.

At the top of the stairs, he glanced toward Hannah's door, wishing it would open and she'd step out. He frowned at the thought. What was wrong with him? He didn't need the interruption. He had enough on his mind.

Turning toward his own door, he unlocked it and stepped inside. For a furnished apartment, it was empty of anything to make it feel like home.

"It'll get better," he murmured, dropping his briefcase on the end of the sofa and pulling his tie off to roll it up and stuff it in the jacket pocket of his suit.

Wandering over to the refrigerator, he opened it out of habit, and then stood staring at…nothing. He'd forgotten to go to the store on the way home. How could he have forgotten to ride the trolley to the end of the next block to get a few staples?

His sigh was deep and long as he slammed the door and, without allowing his body the needed relaxation, headed for the front door.

****

With the new neighbor eating with her the previous evening, there was no left-over food for tonight's supper. Hannah hated shopping, but here she was, back at the store, picking up several items she'd need to make a Minestrone soup and a pot of beans to carry her for the rest of the week. All she needed now was a box of crackers and a half-pound of dry navy beans. Maybe dinner tonight would just be a cheese sandwich. The day had been grueling—and most of it she'd spent on her feet.

"Hey there."

She jerked around at the sound of the familiar, deep voice—the voice that had plagued her dreams and given her a restless night's sleep. "Hi, John."

"I didn't expect to find anyone here who could help me."

"You need help shopping for food?" She frowned

slightly. "Oh, that's right, you don't cook."

"Not much, anyway. I usually make sandwiches and have corn flakes for breakfast."

She'd heard the same story from other single, male tenants over the years. Men really should be taught at least the basics. "So, what do you need help with?"

"I need a couple easy things to make. You know, easy recipes and a crash course in cooking."

Hannah had to chuckle at the picture of this tall, strong male standing in front of a stove with an apron on to protect his nice suit. "I guess I could help you out with a couple recipes."

He paused for a moment as he studied her. "Say, I might have an even better idea. How about my paying for all the groceries needed to make dinner each night, you cook it, and we eat it together?"

Her stomach fluttered. "You're joking, right?" Her chuckle was weak. Could he be asking to spend every evening with her? "I mean, we don't even know each other."

"Am I joking? Well, if you agree, then I wasn't kidding, but if you don't like the idea..." He shrugged, looking as innocent as a child caught with crumbs around his mouth.

She could no longer contain the laughter. "You have quite a sense of humor—not to mention a high level of self-confidence."

"My stepfather told me once that it never hurts to ask."

"Oh, really?" She still couldn't hold back her laughter. "Did you really think I'd agree to such a bold suggestion?"

He picked up several apples and put them in his

bag. "Look at it this way. If I ask and you say yes, great—we both win. However, if you say no, I don't get what I want, but not asking also means I don't get what I want. I have nothing to lose in asking."

"I guess you've got a point," she conceded, seriously considering his proposal.

"You did mention you don't like eating alone...and I noticed that you have yet to tell me no, so can I assume you like my idea?"

She opened her mouth, blinked a couple times, then closed it again. With their gazes locked, she was unable to look away. Held hostage without a touch, she silently debated the situation. She liked his voice, and he worked at Hughes. Good or bad, all she could do was stare up into the hypnotic blue gaze that held her like a fly on sticky paper. True, she hadn't turned him down, but why not? Easy. For the first time since her mother's death, she felt a thrill at the thought of tomorrow. She had enjoyed their meal together the previous evening. The conversation had been light and entertaining, and even when discussing their parents, she'd felt a closeness with John like she'd never felt with another man.

"Well...?" He arched both eyebrows, quirked one side of his mouth up into a mischievous smile, and waited.

She could only stare. Words were locked behind the door where her heart pounded.

"I have a suggestion," he added when she remained silent. "Why don't we try it for a week and see how it goes?"

Her stomach churned. John leaned nonchalantly against a counter where boxes of cereal were artfully stacked. He appeared confident and relaxed, the total opposite of her. She wanted to say yes—wanted to know him better, and actually loved his idea since it would save her money and also mean not being alone every evening, but inner turmoil dredged up barriers. People would talk.

Mother, what should I do?

Her mind whirled with possibilities and potential problems. What if he ended up being like Eddie? Two dates and the guy wouldn't take no for an answer now. Then she weighed the possible problems against having someone to talk with each evening—someone who was nice and polite. Besides, having him there each evening might discourage Eddie, and as she concluded back at the beginning, the trial arrangement would certainly help her budget.

In the end, she threw caution to the wind and made the decision based on what she wanted to do. "Yes. I'm willing to try it for one week."

She couldn't stop the smile that spread slowly, dragging warmth with it to flush her neck and ears. With a hand worrying a button on her dress, she pressed against her chest where a galloping herd of horses thundered across her heart.

"Great."

Excitement wrapped her in a warm glow. She loved his smile, a smile that displayed white teeth against a deeply tanned face. He wore his dark brown hair a little longer than normal on the sides, but it flattered him. *And boy does he look good in a suit.* Even without a tie, as he was now, he belonged up on the big screen.

Then a thought pounced, drawing her shoulders

back and narrowing her eyes to glare at him. "Are you looking to get into movies?"

"What?" His eyes widened as he pushed away from the counter and stood with both hands resting on his hips. "No way. I'm a designer—of planes."

A frown dug a deep groove across his forehead, but gradually faded after she slowly smiled.

"Good." She hesitated, but decided total honesty was the best answer. "I work at Paramount, and sometimes people want an introduction to someone in the industry."

He stared for several more moments before his shoulders relaxed and his own smile returned. "I understand. So," he said, glancing into her bag of groceries, "what meals are you planning?"

"Navy beans with cornbread and vegetable soup."

He nodded. "I'll get some ground beef for a small meat loaf and some potatoes and carrots, okay? And more spaghetti noodles and tomatoes. In fact, why don't you tell me what is needed."

Hannah tingled from head to toe as they wandered along together, putting food in their bags. With the meals planned for the next week, she began to relax.

"And as payment in advance for your cooking skills, can I buy you dinner tonight at the diner on the next corner? It's too late to go home and cook." He set the groceries on the counter and waited for the clerk to write down the cost of each item and add the column. Once he'd paid for the food, they were ready to go.

The pros and cons were quickly weighed, but in the end, she found it impossible to deny this man—especially since she wanted more time with him.

He picked up both bags of food, then patiently

waited for her answer. With doubts and cautions shoved to the recesses of her mind, she nodded, committing herself to following his lead.

Reality lurked, asking why he had chosen her and why everything was happening so fast, but she quickly buried all the doubts and worries. She was walking on a cloud. If only this dream could last forever. Mr. Nolan had told her to find a new beau, so maybe that's what she was doing. She definitely wanted to spend time with John, and that was what mattered most at the moment. Tomorrow was soon enough to listen to reason—and with any luck, tomorrow and reason would never come.

****

John stood at Hannah's apartment door, smiling as he thought about how the first week eating together had gracefully slid into a second and then a third. Every evening, he knocked on her apartment door at seven o'clock. They'd eat, share about their day, and laugh about things said or done at work. Then he'd say goodnight and go home to an empty apartment to sleep. He couldn't ignore his feelings much longer. It became harder each night to leave without holding her hand or kissing her goodnight. Would she even allow it?

He loved the moment she opened the door and smiled before ushering him inside. The anticipation of what she'd be wearing and whether her beautiful long hair would be worn up or down made him laugh and shake his head. This feeling was new, and it left him a bit confused.

"Hey, come on in."

Tonight, her hair hung long and wavy, begging him to run his fingers through its thick length. He shoved his hands into his pockets and stepped inside, hesitating while she shut the door behind him.

"It smells wonderful in here."

"Vegetable soup and cornbread," she told him, grinning from ear to ear. "And I even have a surprise." Without waiting for him to comment, she continued, "I made pudding for dessert."

"Goodness, that's a rare treat. I haven't had pudding in…" He pondered a moment. "Not in over a year at least."

"Oh, and thank you again for the tin of Sanka." She smiled at him over her shoulder as she scooped grounds into the pot. "I was getting a little tired of Postum."

"Treat it like gold. Mr. Hughes was so impressed with my work that he gave the 'little bonus.' I was more excited than if he'd given me an extra ten dollars."

She nodded. "I just wish I had real milk. I've gotten used to the powered kind, but still, it's almost a sin to put it in a cup of real brewed coffee."

"Have you tried drinking it black?"

"Black? Not lately. Maybe I will tonight."

After she set two bowls of soup on the table and a plate with cornbread, he held her chair and then joined her at the table to bless the food and eat. It took only twenty minutes to finish, but he felt he'd monopolized the conversation. When Hannah stood and began gathering dishes, he joined her in the kitchen to wash the few items while she dried and put them away.

"With that chore finished, why don't you relax in the living room while I turn the coffee on to perk? I'll be in shortly."

John sank down on the couch, stretched out his long legs, and flexed his ankle to relieve a slight cramp in his calf from being crammed into a tight cockpit to see for himself just how much room the design allowed the pilot. There had to be a way to allow at least a few more inches...

No, he needed to forget work for now. "Tell me about your day," he said aloud. "I did all the talking during dinner."

She turned and leaned against the kitchen counter, waiting while the coffee brewed. "I find your job more fascinating than mine—especially all the stories about Mr. Hughes. Of course, I hear stories about him down at Paramount, but they're about upcoming movies or which leading lady he's dating now. He leads such a varied and interesting life."

John respected his boss' brilliance and business sense, but as far as his personal life outside the plant, the man didn't appear to be very faithful. He wined and dined different ladies as if he couldn't make up his mind, or maybe he didn't want to be shackled to only one.

That definitely wasn't what John wanted out of life. He wanted...well, that remained to be seen.

He glanced up when Hannah set the two cups on the coffee table and sat in the chair to his side. This evening, she'd changed into slacks and a white, tailored blouse, reminding him of Katharine Hepburn and making her look slender and taller than usual, even though she stood no more than a few inches over five feet.

She slipped off her shoes and propped her feet on the rungs under the coffee table. He could see red polish on her toenails, giving his stomach an odd, jumbled feeling—as if he'd peeked into her bedroom.

He now knew something personal that the rest of the world didn't know. To hide his discomfort, he reached for the coffee and sipped in silence, fighting an urge to ask her to move to the couch and join him.

No. That would put temptation within arm's reach. Too close.

"As for how my day went, it was much the same. They're still working on *The Trail of the Lonesome Pine* with Henry Fonda, Fred MacMurray, and Sylvia Sidney, but I'd only get to do her hair in an emergency. I did Beulah Bondi's make-up once, but, of course, I usually do the extras." She lowered her gaze to the coffee, her lips drooping just before she sipped the hot brew.

"Hannah, you're young and just starting out. I'm sure you'll become well-known and sought-after in time."

A thought darted through his mind that stopped his next sentence before it could be spoken. If he casually mentioned her to Mr. Hughes and where she worked, he might see to it she got the chance to realize her dream.

And then it slammed into him—he had just considered doing exactly what he hadn't wanted Vince to do for him. Interfere.

No, he'd keep his mouth shut. If she was good enough to rise to the top, she'd know she was there on her own effort. He wouldn't sneak around behind her back.

A gentle smile touched her lips before she lifted her gaze to meet his. "You're sweet. But that wasn't what was making me feel a little melancholy. I was thinking about my mother and how she was robbed of having the chance to live out her dream, see me married some day, and eventually see her grandchildren. She'll miss out on so much."

He found it difficult to understand women. Their emotions were so much more tender and so much closer to the surface. Dealing with a sad woman was like walking through a field riddled with land mines—an explosion could occur at any step.

The best plan of action was to remain quiet, but he couldn't stop himself from leaning over to place a hand on her arm. A simple touch always seemed to make his mother feel better.

Her skin felt chilled under his hand. Before he thought, he slid it down to clasp hers and tug. "Why don't you come over here and sit with me. You're cold."

Hannah remained motionless for several moments, her brows tightened in a slight frown. Then she stood, pulling her hand from under his. She remained standing, staring down into his upturned face, and then walked around the coffee table to ease down beside him on the sofa.

His heart pounded like a carpenter's hammer. Was she really going to allow him to provide comfort and warmth? Blood rushed past his ears, drowning out the soft music currently playing on the radio. His breath caught behind the blockage in his throat, and he swallowed several times. This was a pivotal moment— a moment he hadn't prepared for.

She sat next to him, yet remained at least a foot away. Did he dare push her to move a little closer? He reached out, grasped her hand, and tugged gently. After a hesitation and a glance from under long lashes, she scooted a few inches closer. That's all the encouragement he needed. He moved the rest of the way until his arm pressed up against hers. Then he squeezed her hand and reached over to run a finger along her knuckle's bumpy ridges and valleys.

"You're very beautiful. Especially when you're embarrassed," he added, chuckling even as he held firm when she inched away. "Hey, don't go. I was only teasing and hoping to lighten the mood." He wove his fingers between hers, meshing their palms together, then sent up a silent thanks when her shoulders sagged and she leaned against him.

"I guess I don't take teasing well," she admitted, glancing at him before quickly looking away to pick at a thread on her slacks. "My mother and I laughed a lot, but there wasn't much joking around. I guess life—just existing—was too much of a struggle to leave time for that."

"With the ongoing depression, I know a lot of people have lost everything. I probably didn't think as much about it because I was busy studying at college."

"From what I hear, it's tougher in some areas of the country than others, but no one has escaped the impact. At least we can have meat once in a while, even if it's outrageously expensive, but things are looking a little better each month. At least according to the radio news reports."

"True. We're very fortunate to have jobs so we can afford the basics."

"When they're available," she added with a quick smile.

He opened his hand, putting their palms together. She was tiny as a minute by comparison. It suddenly sent thoughts of protecting her flashing through his mind, which sent thoughts of Vince trailing close behind. Again, he regretted the agreement to keep the don informed on how she was doing.

Well, that wasn't going to happen, so it was better not to think about it.

"My mother always said things would get better, that America always rises to the occasion and does whatever is necessary—like during the recent world war." Her gaze remained on their hands. "Never forget the Lusitania," she murmured.

"No, I don't think anyone ever will. At least I know I won't. I just wish it hadn't taken the death of so many people to motivate America to get involved in the battle. Anyway, your mother must have been a wise woman."

Hannah nodded. "I miss her. She was always preaching to me about women's rights, and how the suffrage movement was a vital step in gaining equality with men, but she refused several offers to speak at public meetings on behalf of the cause." She glanced toward him before she continued, "I think that's why I enjoy having you here in the evening. We can talk about anything—even political events. Also…"

She began to pull her hand from his, but he tightened his grip. "What is it? What's wrong?"

"Um, well, I need to admit something that I—that is a bit embarrassing. I hope you won't hate me for it." She kept her chin lowered, refusing to meet his gaze.

"Tell me." He made sure his voice was gentle, but firm. He needed to know what was troubling her.

"Oh, it's nothing, really, but…"

He tugged gently on her hand in encouragement.

"Okay. There's this guy at work—one of the

lighting technicians—who took me to a show once and dinner once, but now he keeps asking me to go out with him, and he's beginning to make me feel uneasy. I keep saying no, but he's persistent. Yesterday, I told him I'm seeing someone else. You," she added after a hesitation. She glanced up at him from beneath her lashes before jerking her gaze away.

She told someone—someone who apparently isn't taking no for an answer—that she's dating me?

How was he supposed to feel about this new wrinkle? He stared at the beautiful woman who had instantly caught his attention the day he arrived. Okay, so the guy now thought *he* was Hannah's guy.

Good.

"What did he say about your announcement?"

"Not much. He just asked who you were and if I've known you for very long, but I didn't tell him anything. It's none of his business."

John nodded, but a thought nagged. Just the thought of some other guy paying attention to Hannah made his jaws clench. Jealousy?

No. Well, maybe.

But still, something was making him want to tell the guy to shove off and leave her alone.

Admit it, you're falling for her.

That thought brought his mind skidding to an abrupt halt.

Really?

The more he thought about it, the more sense it made. Still wanting to deny the dawning truth, he mentally argued with himself. His plans hadn't included coming to care about Hannah, and definitely didn't include him falling in love with her, despite the first jolt he'd felt when he looked into her eyes several weeks earlier.

"John?"

"Hmm?" He blinked and then focused on those eyes—eyes narrowed by a frown. "Oh, sorry, I was just thinking about the guy. What's his name?"

"Eddie Stone. He's harmless, just a nuisance."

"Well, let me know if he keeps bothering you."

"Why?" she asked, chuckling. "Will you go rough him up and tell him to stay away?"

"Something like that," he replied, laughing along with her, but more serious than he'd been in his life.

If this man meant her any harm, he'd go to the mat to stand between her and danger. If she only knew what he was capable of—what Vince had taught him about self-defense and what he'd learned about wrestling and boxing while at college. She'd probably be frightened enough to tell him to leave. His fighting abilities were also something he'd kept from his mother, and something else he'd need to keep from Hannah.

Which brought his mind full-circle. Although he'd never actually lied to her, he hated how he was becoming a pro at skirting around the truth.

"How about that pudding?"

Her eyes lit up. "Sounds good."

He watched her rise and head to the kitchen, but his mind continued to churn. Of course, he hadn't told her that he was technically doing a favor for her real father by keeping an eye on her, but now he began to see why her father felt she needed watching. She was alone in the world, vulnerable.

John narrowed his eyes and lifted his chin a notch at the thought of anyone bothering her. With God as his witness, he'd do whatever was necessary to protect her—and it had nothing to do with what his stepfather might think was owed him.

Even though he refused to let her father pay him, he had just found out his rent was paid that month. He planned to contact Vince and tell him he would pay his own way, but the man was stubborn. He'd just have to be adamant. If he lived rent-free, Vince had control—the same as if he were on the man's payroll.

Guilt welled up and threatened to suffocate him, but what could he do? There was always the option of moving to another apartment, but he now knew he needed to stay close in order to take care of Hannah. He mulled over the option of telling the truth and letting the chips fall wherever they fell, but immediately dismissed it—at least for the time being.

"Here we go," she said, handing him the small dish of pudding.

Vanilla with cinnamon sprinkled on top. Different...but good, he decided after taking a bite. Maybe the old adage about the way to a man's heart had some truth to it. If he let his guard down, this woman could tie him in knots. Of course, there was a huge problem with that scenario. He'd either have to keep secrets from her for the rest of their lives, or he'd have to tell her the truth about her father and, consequently, expose her mother's lies.

The thought of shattering Hannah's memories of her mother made his stomach muscles tighten. He had quite the quandary now—he either continued a life of lies, keeping the truth from the woman he was falling in love with, or he told the truth and risked shattering their budding relationship.

He ate in silence while the dilemma dragged his former good mood down to his feet. What should he do? What *could* he do? The choices were to betray a promise to Vince or betray Hannah's growing trust.

Either way, he lost.

Chapter Five

Hannah had a new vitality, a new bounce to her step, and she didn't care who noticed. John had held her hand and hadn't even gotten angry when she confessed using his name to get Eddie to stop asking her out. She'd been a little wary at work, but the lighting technician had stayed away, as if he accepted she was dating someone else.

As if a cherry had been added to her sundae, today, she and John were having meat with their dinner. He had gotten a half-pound of ground beef, and she fixed spaghetti with meat balls for dinner. She'd cooked all the meat, adding a small onion for flavor, but they'd only be eating half tonight. With the other half in the refrigerator for another night.

In the pocket of her sweater was all the rent money except from Mr. Nolan. Best she could figure, she barely had the five minutes to stop by his apartment. Her hand was raised to knock when John entered the lobby.

"Hey, pretty lady."

She loved how he'd started greeting her. Working with movie stars all day tended to leave her feeling bland and unexciting. He had a way of brightening the day and making her believe what he said.

"Hey, yourself. I have one more rent to collect, and then we can go up. Dinner is ready."

"Wonderful. Today was grueling, and I missed lunch. But while I'm thinking about it, I have something to ask you."

She turned to face him, still wondering how she happened to get such a handsome tenant who was so kind and generous. He had her full attention. "Sure. What is it?"

"I can't believe my luck," he started, taking her hand and smiling down into her eyes. "I'm new at Hughes Aircraft, but I've been invited to cocktails and dinner at a party my boss is hosting this Saturday—and I can bring a guest. Would you like to join me?"

Her heart thudded, then raced as she reached out to grab his arm. John could have asked anyone, but he'd chosen her.

"Are you kidding?" Joy bubbled up and overflowed in a smile she couldn't seem to wipe from her face. She didn't even care that she sounded like a child being offered a special prize. "I can't believe it. I've seen him at the studio, at a distance, but never up close—never so close that I could reach out and touch him," she added, a giggle slipping out.

"Do you have something to wear to a cocktail party?"

"No...yes," she amended, thrilled at the memory of her mother's blue dress hanging in the back of her closet.

Thank you, Mom.

"Wonderful. Now, let's hurry and get Mr. Nolan's rent so we can have dinner. I'm starved." He squeezed her hand just before releasing it.

Hannah turned away and knocked on the apartment door. "Since you missed lunch, you'll love what we're having."

"Come in," came the muffled call.

John followed her inside. She could well imagine what Mr. Nolan would say about him being with her. He'd already hinted that the new tenant "was cut from a good bolt of cloth."

The older man's face lit when he saw them enter. "Why, stars alive. Hannah, honey, I think you latched onto a keeper this time." Then he added an exaggerated wink.

"Mr. Nolan, you're a mess." She glanced over her shoulder before turning back to the man. Thankfully, John was laughing. "Have you met John Staples?"

"Seen him leaving for work in the mornings and spoke to him once." He reached out to shake. "My mind's a bit fuzzy. Where did you say you're from, boy?"

"Mobile, Alabama."

"Thought I detected the accent," he announced, cackling when he laughed. "Can spot 'em every time. I've always loved the way people talk down in the deep South."

Hannah smiled over at John, noting his lack of embarrassment. "Um," she started, turning back to the elderly man. "I'm here for the rent, and we're in a bit of a rush, but I thought you might find it interesting that John works over at Hughes Aircraft. He designs planes." She knew the warmth around her neck meant her face had flushed a deep pink—a dead give-away that she saw John as special, and something her tenant wouldn't miss.

The older man grinned, then turned his gaze toward him. "So he told me when we met. Got us another engineer. Designed and built bridges in my day," he said, nodding.

Hannah had listened to the man's stories and knew how proud he was about his accomplishments.

"We'll have to talk sometime, young man." He reached out to shake hands again. "Yes, a definite keeper," he added with another wink in her direction. "Rent payment is over on the counter."

Hannah picked up the money, then gave the older man a quick wave before leaving with John and heading upstairs. "Isn't he a card?"

"I can tell he's fond of you, and I look forward to talking with him one of these days. He's the kind of man I wish I'd had for a grandfather while growing up. I bet he has a lot of knowledge to share."

"I've known him all my life, and I've always seen him as a grandfather. I didn't have a father or grandparents, so he filled the void." She unlocked her apartment door and led the way in. "I'll need about three or four minutes to warm the meal. Why don't you turn on the radio and relax until it's ready?"

"I'll set the table."

John had talked a bit about his mama, but already, Hannah knew she'd like the woman. Anyone who taught a young man to help out in the kitchen was okay in her book.

"You and your mother look so much alike."

She glanced around to see him holding the photo, staring intently at it. "Yes. Isn't she lovely?"

"You look like sisters in this picture."

"Thank you. Mother said I have my father's eyes—and the shape of his toes," she said, laughing softly. "She was very young when she had me, and then with my father being killed in the line of duty, she was left with the huge responsibility of raising me alone." She struck a match and used it to light the stove's gas burner under the pot of spaghetti.

"You said there's no other family, right?"

She shook her head.

"Not even any fellow police officers coming by to help out?"

Again, she shook her head. She'd often wondered why she had no family and why her mother never dated or remarried. The one time she'd asked, the answer had been vague. Something about there being one who came by every so often to check on her after she'd given birth, but then he'd gone into the Army, and she'd never seen him again. She hadn't asked again until her late teens, and then the answer had been simple and understandable. The love she had for her deceased husband was still strong, and she'd never dishonor him. Her mother's story would have made a great movie.

John returned the picture to its spot and set the table by the time the green beans and spaghetti were hot.

Very little was said during dinner. Hannah's mind had been thrust back in time, making it difficult to carry on a regular conversation. There were so many unanswered questions. She knew almost nothing about her extended family. She'd always wondered if the families had been against the marriage or if her mother had gotten pregnant before getting married, so everyone had looked down on her. Now, the answers were buried forever.

Guilt kept John quiet during dinner. Sadie

Montgomery had made her fake husband out to be a hero any little girl could be proud to call Daddy—a man totally opposite of the one who gave Hannah life.

He took a long drink of water, keeping his gaze downcast. The situation was only getting worse as time went on. The problem lay in knowing the truth—keeping an important truth from someone was nothing more than lying, and he hated lying to her.

His contempt for Vince grew daily. How could the man treat him like a son one minute and put him in a position to spy on someone the next?

Then reality settled in.

No, I can't blame him. I agreed to the suggestion. It's my own fault.

In the middle of berating himself for being stupid, the wall phone out in the hall began to ring.

"Oh, I have to get that. Be right back."

He watched her dart out the door. Before the third ring, he heard her answer the call.

"Hello? Yes, ma'am. Actually, he's right here. Please hold on."

John pushed the chair back and was already standing when she entered the apartment.

"The call is for you. It's your mother."

"Thanks." He stepped into the hall and pulled the door almost closed behind him. "Hi, Mother. How are you?" He pressed the receiver to his ear, trying to hear her over the static on the line.

"Hi, Johnny. I'm fine, but I haven't heard from you in a month of Sundays. I just needed to know you're okay way out there in California."

He leaned against the wall and closed his eyes. "I'm fine. Work is good, and my apartment is great."

"Are you eating enough?"

"You'll be happy to know I've struck a deal with Hannah, my landlady. I buy some of the food, and she cooks my dinner every night."

Despite the youthful-sounding Hannah having answered the phone, he knew his mother like the back of his hand. She'd assume the young woman was a neighbor—not the manager of a boardinghouse. No, she'd picture a plump, older lady, and him eating the prepared food in his own apartment—alone.

Now wasn't the time to enlighten her.

"Oh, I'm relieved to hear that."

He held the phone, waiting for her to continue, but all he heard was static. "Mother? Are you still there?"

"Yes, I'm here. I'm trying to find a good way to ask you about Vince."

"Vince?" He straightened. "What does he have to do with anything?"

"I didn't want to tell you this, but I've seen a guy hanging around lately, and I wanted to be sure he has nothing to do with your stepfather checking up on me."

"I doubt that—not after all these years." Still, John didn't like the sound of someone hanging around his mother. He'd have to be sure to call and ask.

"Okay, I won't worry about it."

"If I were you, I wouldn't worry, but I'd keep my eyes open and be careful."

"That makes sense."

She was too quiet. This didn't sound like his mother. "Do you want me to tell you one more time that I'm not working for him?"

"Would you tell me if you were?"

She had a point, but it still saddened him to have

her doubt his word. "I work for Howard Hughes. Period."

He waited, but she remained silent. It didn't take a genius to realize his mother needed something—needed him. This issue wasn't going to be settled over the phone. Mr. Hughes had invited him to join a meeting in Atlanta, Georgia, the following week, and if he could arrange to go a day or two early, he could stop off in Alabama and talk with her face-to-face.

With the decision made, his shoulders relaxed. "Mother, I have to fly to Atlanta next week, if I can arrange it, I'll come for a quick visit. We can talk more then, okay?"

Silence.

"Are you still there?"

"Yes. I'd *love* to see you. I'll look forward to it."

"Talk to you then. Love you."

"Love you, too."

John stood staring at the box hanging on the wall long after he hung up the receiver. What was going on? Without wasting time, he dialed the operator and gave her the number in New York. It took a few minutes, but after going through their security process, Vince soon came on the line.

"Hey, boy. How's it going out your way?"

"Hi. I'm fine, but in a hurry, so I'll get right to the point. First, I'll be paying my own rent from now on," he began pointedly. "Second, I need to know if you have someone watching my mother." His heart thundered, beating numerous times before his stepfather finally spoke.

"I won't lie to you. Yes, I have someone keeping an eye on her—always have. Why?"

"She knows about it—noticed the guy—and she's afraid."

A heavy sigh crossed the line. "I'll take care of it. I don't want her frightened."

"Thanks. I have to go. Talk with you soon."

"Hey…"

John hung up the phone, not wanting to get into a discussion about Hannah or the rent issue. Did Vince have someone watching him? He stood with his head leaned back against the wall and eyes closed, drawing several deep breaths and releasing them slowly before he turned and entered Hannah's apartment.

"Everything okay?"

"Yeah. My mother just wanted to be sure I was okay and eating enough." He joined her when she laughed.

"Well, I can't blame her. If I had a son living a couple thousand miles away, I'd probably worry a little bit, too." She stood to clear the coffee table. "You left the apartment door open, so I couldn't help but hear you mention the name, Vince. Is that a relative of yours?"

Her question slammed into his chest. He took an extra few moments to pick up his dishes and follow her into the kitchen, giving himself time to decide what to say. "Not really. It's someone my mother knows." *Liar, liar, liar.*

"Will you get to see him when you visit your mother next week?"

"No, he doesn't live in Alabama." *At least that's the truth.*

She stood absently staring toward the dishes, her hands motionless on the edge of the sink. "You know,

I'd love to see this country. I've never been outside Los Angeles."

"I would, too, but I'd want to drive. I flew here from Alabama, so I saw only clouds." Setting the dishes on the counter, he turned to lean back against the cupboard, casually sticking his hands into the pockets of his slacks. "Where would you like to visit?"

Hannah ran water into the sink and added detergent, swishing it around to make bubbles before she put the dishes and coffee cups in to soak.

"I'd love to see the Grand Canyon, for one thing, and the East coast. I'm told the shores along the Atlantic Ocean are totally different from the Pacific Ocean shoreline. Have you been to many states?"

"Alabama, Arkansas, New Jersey, New York, and California," he answered, ticking off fingers of one hand.

"*Five* states. Goodness, that's exciting. Oh, I'd love to visit New York, too, and see a show on Broadway."

"I can understand your interest, but Broadway was adversely affected when the talking movies started."

"Do you think it'll kill the stage industry?" She handed him a plate to dry.

"I doubt it. Everyone loves theater. There's something special about seeing a play where the people act out the show live."

She tilted her head slightly and stared at him. "It sounds like you enjoy the stage."

"My mother used to take me before…well, before she left my stepfather and moved back to Mobile."

She finished washing the rest of the dishes, unplugged the sink, and allowed the soapy water to run down the drain. "Did you get along with your stepdad?"

"Oh yeah." He set the dried dishes on the cupboard shelf before continuing. "He was always very good to me."

"What was he like?"

John swallowed. He was digging himself into a hole. "The man is a deep and colorful story that will take a while to tell. Can I get into him another time? I have some blueprints I need to go over this evening."

He hung the dish towel on the peg near the stove and headed to the door while she trailed behind. Before stepping out into the hall, he turned and smiled down into her upturned face. He couldn't miss the disappointment in her expressive, blue eyes.

He hesitated, almost changing his mind, but the urge to distance himself from her questions overrode any guilt. "Don't forget about tomorrow night. Hughes is sending a car at six o'clock to take us to the Beverly Hills Hotel." Thankfully, her eyes lit up, and a broad smile spread across her face. His shoulders relaxed.

"Oh, John, I'm so excited about the party. I've heard about that hotel, even ridden past it, and I'm dying to see inside."

Her enthusiasm and joy at the outing made him feel good, but going home early meant some long, lonely hours before going to bed. He'd miss listening to her soft voice and seeing her shy smiles over the rim of her coffee cup. She was exciting—but she was Vince's daughter.

That fact must never be forgotten.

He beat a hasty retreat, glad to be off the hot seat and away from her curiosity about Vince.

At least for the moment.

Chapter Six

Hannah sank onto the sofa and released a deep sigh into the silence shrouding the room. She'd gotten used to spending a couple of hours talking with John over dinner and coffee. It really didn't matter what they talked about, but they usually started with sharing the events of their day.

"I don't understand why a call from his mother changed the mood and ended the evening so abruptly." Her words whispered out as she wrapped both arms around a small crocheted pillow, hugging it against her stomach. "Or was it my questions about the guy, Vince, that changed the course of the evening?"

She tossed the pillow aside, stood, and walked listlessly toward the kitchen. She didn't normally listen to conversations on the phone outside her apartment, but he'd left the door partially open. There had been no way to miss his side of the conversation.

She stooped to get the dust rag from under the sink. Keeping her hands busy with the menial task didn't stop her mind from obsessing about John's confusing yet intriguing words on the phone.

His reaction to her question was what made her so curious. *Who is Vince?*

Apparently not a relative, but then he'd hung up and made another call, asking the person on the other end if someone was watching his mother. Strange, but then he'd shared that his mother knew and was afraid. Her hand stilled halfway along the table. Had he been talking to the police?

What if someone were following her? A chill ran down her arms. Low in her stomach, acid churned. Involuntarily, her hand came up to press against the pain. Did John's early departure really have to do with work or was he just avoiding her questions?

Hannah's thoughts came to an abrupt halt when the hall phone rang again. She left the rag on the table and hurried out to grab it on the second ring. "Hello?"

"Hannah, it's Eddie. How are you?"

Ugh. She grimaced even as she closed her eyes and leaned back against the wall. "Oh, hi."

"Well, don't sound so enthusiastic." He chuckled. "You sound a little down-in-the-mouth, but I know how to cheer you up."

She knew he'd called to ask her out—and that she'd be turning him down. She hated this part of dating.

When she remained silent, he finally continued, "There's a new movie at The Gem Theater, and I'm taking you out for an evening. You need to be cheered up."

Her mother had always said the best way to handle a problem was to face it and be specific with your answer. Yes or no, without hemming or hawing. "It's nice of you to think of me b—"

"Great. Why don't I pick you up tomorrow, and we can get something to eat first?"

She sighed. Eddie had definitely become a problem. *Be specific.* "No, Eddie. Like I told you before, I'm seeing someone else now, so I can't go out with you. Thanks anyway, though."

The silence lasted several seconds. Had no one ever turned him down before?

"Are you sure? Who's the guy? Someone from work?"

"No one you know. He's new to town. Listen, I have to go. I have some work to do."

"Sure, see you."

Hannah hung up the receiver, knowing in her heart Eddie would probably continue to call. Why had she thought telling him there was another guy would make a difference?

She shook her head, remembering the day he announced to their co-workers that they were a couple.

Hopefully, being told no will take care of things.

Regardless, thank goodness she'd mentioned to John that she'd used his name; in case they ran into Eddie at the store or something, John wouldn't be caught off-guard. Hopefully this would discourage the overt lighting technician.

She glanced over her shoulder just before entering her apartment and closing the door. *John's poor mother.* Is this what it felt like to be followed—looking over your shoulder and wondering if anyone was watching what you do? The shudder darted down her back, making her shiver and raising chill bumps on her arms.

To get her mind off Eddie, she quickly finished dusting and then went to her closet and pulled out the midnight-blue cocktail dress. In front of the dresser mirror, she held it before her with one hand and swept her hair up with her other.

"Earrings. I need earrings."

After carefully hanging the dress back in the closet, she slipped into her mother's room and lifted the lid of the box sitting front and center on the dresser. Wrapped in a thin, embroidered hankie were her mother's pride and joy. When an actress had worn the long, dangling diamond earrings onto the set, her mother had told her the jewelry made her look lovely. The young woman had taken them off and given them to her. Just like that. Two months later, the wardrobe mistress divulged the earrings weren't stage jewelry, but real diamonds, a gift from one of the star's former admirers.

"Okay, that's settled. I'll wear mother's slinky blue dress, the diamond earrings, and her silver heels. And I'll do something special with my hair. Perfect," she whispered, re-wrapping the jewelry and returning it to the box.

With nothing else to occupy her thoughts, she spent the next half-hour pondering John. Was he keeping secrets from his mother?

Could he also be keeping secrets from me?

After all, when he called the police—or whomever he'd called—he hadn't given any explanations or his mother's address. No information at all. He'd only told the person she suspected she was being followed. Was John in on it? But why would he have his mother followed?

Thoughts raced across her mind, retreated, and then settled in to marinate. No, he wouldn't—couldn't—hurt his own mother. She shook her head at the very thought of such a thing. He was too gentle, too considerate.

Still, something wasn't right. Should she ask him if his mother was in danger? Technically, it was none of her business, but… Her fingers tightened into fists.

The phone ringing again jolted her from her thoughts. Once again, she slipped out into the hall and lifted the receiver after the second ring. "Hello?"

After a momentary hesitation, the caller spoke. "Is this Hannah?"

"Yes, ma'am."

"Hello, dear. I called earlier. I'm John's mother. So, you're the manager there?"

"Yes, ma'am, and good evening, Mrs. Staples."

"Goodness, you sound rather young to be managing a boardinghouse."

"My mother used to be manager, but when she passed recently, I took over."

"I'm so sorry. That must have been awful for you."

"Yes, ma'am, but it's getting better with time," she lied.

"Well, dear, I'm glad to have a chance to thank you for cooking for my Johnny. He can't boil water without burning it," she said with an airy chuckle. "And please, call me Grace."

Hannah felt an instant connection. The first time she heard the woman's voice, she'd known immediately the caller was John's mother. The southern accent was strong and distinctive, and Mrs. Staples' cheerful personality was so much like her own mother's outlook on life.

"Thank you. You're very kind. And as to cooking for John, it's no problem. I enjoy his company. Living alone can get lonely."

A soft sigh came over the wire. "Yes, I learned that when he went away to college."

Several silent seconds ticked by. "Um, if you'll hold on just a moment, I'll check and see if he's home."

"Thank you."

With the receiver perched on top of the phone, she turned toward John's apartment. After two knocks, she figured he was either not at home or choosing not to answer the door. She hoped the call wasn't important enough for him to miss.

The urge to tell his mother what she'd overheard earlier was sudden and strong. Should she get involved? He wouldn't appreciate her intruding in whatever was going on, yet, what if Mrs. Staples *was* in danger? If Hannah kept what she heard to herself and then learned later that the woman had been injured or kidnapped, or…or worse, she'd never forgive herself.

Eyes closed, heart pounding, and decision made, she gripped the receiver. "Mrs. Staples, he's not answering, but I'll leave a note under his door letting him know you called." She hesitated.

"Okay, thank you."

"Mrs. Staples…Grace…before you hang up, there's one other thing I need to tell you." Why was she always so impulsive? She'd started the conversation without planning out exactly what to say. She might regret the decision later, but for now, it seemed the right thing to do.

"Certainly, dear. Is everything all right?"

Would his mother tell her to mind her own business? With fingers crossed, she plunged forward. "I know this is none of my business, but I'm concerned about you."

There was a momentary hesitation on the other end of the wire.

"Oh, there's no need to be concerned about me." Grace's voice didn't sound upset when she finally responded to the rather abrupt statement. "I assume you're referring to my feeling that someone is following me? Don't worry. After telling John, I realized how silly it all sounds. Why would anyone care about a woman in her forties?"

Hannah swallowed, already feeling disloyal to John for what she was about to share. "Mrs. Staples, I probably shouldn't say this, but after your son hung up talking to you, he called someone and asked if you were being followed." The long silence made her uncomfortable, but she'd gone too far to stop now. "I don't know what response he got, but John told the person you had noticed and were afraid." Her own heart raced; she could only imagine what the older lady must be thinking and feeling, but she wanted her to be aware…just in case.

The seconds ticked by while she waited for a response.

"Um, did you discuss that conversation with John?"

"I tried. He was vague and then left. We usually…well, he seemed withdrawn and distracted. Do you know why he would tell the person about your call tonight?"

Over the constant hum of static, she could hear the other woman's rapid breathing. Hannah placed a hand over her stomach and pressed.

When she'd just about given up on getting a response, the woman answered.

"Yes, I think so. It was probably… There was a man in my life once who Johnny might have called. His name is Vince, but as to why he would call him, I don't really know. I thought he had severed relations with the man."

Now even more worried, she gripped the phone until her hand cramped. "Why would this Vince guy be following you?"

"He wouldn't do it himself—he'd have someone else do it, but as to why, I don't know. That's a question for John."

"Is Vince John's father?"

"No. He's someone I knew later on. There's a whole long story there, but something you might better hear from my son."

Obviously someone she didn't want to talk about, but someone who was dangerous if he was having the other woman watched. John's stepfather?

She began to tremble. "Okay, but please be careful. I hate the thought of someone following you." Hannah wrapped the cord around her finger, wishing there was something she could do to help. "I know I'm a long distance from you, but if there is ever anything I can do, please let me know."

"You sound like a very sweet young lady, but there's nothing you can do. Just take care of yourself, and be careful who you trust in life. That's all I can say."

She frowned. What was the woman saying? Or was she talking in generalities because of being young and living alone in Los Angeles?

"Okay. Thanks. Bye." She slowly hung up the phone, refocusing her gaze to the scuffed wooden floor while her thoughts whirled. Instead of easing her mind at warning the woman, she was more concerned now than before. Was Grace cautioning her about maybe also being followed? Or could she possibly have been cautioning her in regard to John?

"Naw," she whispered, shaking her head as she stepped inside her apartment and locked the door.

John appeared so aboveboard and honest. He'd never be mixed up with anyone bad—certainly not anyone who'd sneak around like a spy in one of Paramount's movies.

Right?

Chapter Seven

The banging interrupted John's concentration. Saturday morning was his time to sleep an extra hour and then catch up on his reading after a leisurely breakfast. His walk last night after he left Hannah's had helped enough that he had only a slightly fitful night's sleep.

The pounding stopped, but although the knocking wasn't at his door, he laid down the book and went to check out the disturbance. Across the hall, a man stood knocking at Hannah's apartment.

"Excuse me, mister. She's not home."

The guy whirled around, glaring at first, but quickly hiding his irritation behind a forced smile. "Do you know where I can find her?"

"No. Can I give her a message?" Was this the Eddie who was bothering her at work? His hand curled into a fist at his side. When the other man frowned and shook his head, John continued, "She left a little while ago, but I can tell her you came by."

Dark eyebrows dipped again. "Did she go out with her new boyfriend?"

"I don't know that either. May I ask who you are?" His patience was growing thin, but he needed to be certain if he were going to take a stand against whoever had stressed Hannah enough to make her lie about being in a relationship with someone else.

"Just a friend. So, was she alone?"

"I just heard her door shut when she left. I don't keep tabs on her. Do you want me to tell her you were here?"

"No, I'll see her later." He turned and stomped down the stairs without further comment, slamming the outside door when he left the boardinghouse.

John clenched his jaws, his irritation fueling the urge to slam the apartment door. The irritating man *had* to be Eddie Stone, the persistent suitor, but he'd have to wait until Hannah returned to know for sure. He closed his eyes, released a deep sigh, and closed his door with an almost-silent click.

He returned to his book but was no longer able to concentrate. The man had been angry but tried to cover up his emotions. A visiting professor had once lectured on the different types of personalities, including those who had obsessive tendencies and would force themselves or their ideas on someone else. Could this be the case with the well-dressed but angry man? Regardless, divulging information about her to a stranger—particularly an angry stranger—would never happen.

John tried to read again, but the sound of a door being unlocked and opened across the hall drew his attention. Without taking time to mark his page, he tossed the book onto the sofa as he bolted up and opened the hall door before Hannah could step inside her apartment. "Hey."

She glanced over a shoulder, smiled, and cocked her head to the side. "Hey, yourself. Why not come over? I have this really good coffee someone brought me, and it won't take long to make a couple cups."

He followed her in, taking the grocery bag from her arms and heading to the refrigerator. "I'll put these away while you do the coffee."

"Sure, but you'll be happy to know—"

"Real milk!" He held the two bottles up like trophies, smiling at the thought of having such a treat for their coffee. "Lady, you hit the jackpot."

Hannah laughed out loud. "I was just going to tell you about that. I was able to get two, so you can have one for your morning cereal."

"Now that's something I'll look forward to."

After he put one on the counter and the other in the refrigerator, he turned and leaned against the counter to watch her. She moved with such grace—a fluid motion that reminded him of a swan gliding across the water.

"I noticed it didn't take you very long to shop. Guess there weren't many people in the grocers?"

"Actually, the store was crowded, although no one bought a lot."

"Did you have enough money to cover the groceries?"

"I spent three dollars, but there's still a little left from the amount you gave me at the first of the week."

John pulled out his wallet and laid a few more dollars on the counter, then took coffee cups from the cupboard and added a dollop of milk to each one. "I put a little extra money here—you'll need it for next week's food." She glanced over and nodded, but continued to fill the coffee pot with water so he ventured, "Also, you had a visitor earlier."

He watched her face, hoping to see her reaction. She only set the pot on the stove and turned to spoon coffee grounds into the basket.

"Oh?" Her focus remained on making the coffee.

"A guy, a little older than me, was pounding on your door. He didn't give me his name." He frowned when her hand stopped in mid-scoop, her body suddenly tense.

"What did he look like?"

"About six foot, black hair, and dressed nice."

Her shoulders and arms sagged as if her body had deflated. "He's the one I told you about." She resumed making coffee with hands that now trembled. "Eddie."

His back straightened, every muscle tense, ready to protect Hannah against the non-present enemy. The temptation to lash out was strong, but he understood the need to control any rash reaction that would probably have her running from him as fast as possible.

He drew in a breath to the count of ten and released it just as slowly. Better. "Is he bothering you?"

"No, not really," she said, her voice soft. "Like I told you before, I made the mistake of going out with him a couple times, and now it's like he thinks we're engaged or something." She turned around and leaned back against the counter, arms crossed and lips tightened.

"I repeat, is he bothering you?"

She glanced away, eventually shaking her head. John could feel blood pulsating at his temples. If the guy would only return while he was home, he'd love to practice some of Vince's little tricks on the joker for causing Hannah grief.

She slowly dragged her gaze back to meet his. With her chin lowered, she watched him from under her lashes for several moments before speaking. "Can we talk about something else?"

The request came with a hint of pleading. He wanted to give in, not push the issue, but he had to know. "Has he been here before?"

"Can this discussion wait until we have our coffee?"

The tension between them choked off further conversation. He shoved both hands into his pockets and silently fumed.

Hannah eventually poured their coffee, handed one to John, and led the way to the table. Once they were seated, she wrapped her hands around the porcelain cup, took a deep breath, and began. "I told him a couple months ago that I didn't want to date him anymore. He came over once after that—to change my mind."

He clenched his teeth. "What happened?"

With her gaze downcast, she turned the cup around and around in the saucer.

When she failed to answer, he reached across and took one of her hands in his, gentling his tone. "Tell me."

She shrugged, glanced up at him, then lowered her gaze again. "Not a lot, really. It happened before you arrived. When I opened the door, he pushed his way in and started telling me how much he loved me and how he wouldn't take no for an answer. He pushed me up against the wall and was yelling in my face when the former tenant from across the hall pounded on my door. I was able to shove him away and answered. Without my even having to say a word, he came in and threw the guy out."

"Did you know the tenant very well?"

She shook her head. "No, not really. Only by name. He was a writer, so he rarely came out of the apartment."

Vince had obviously been right about needing someone to watch out for his daughter, just not for the reason, or from the people, he'd been concerned about.

"This was right after your mother died, right?"

She nodded, wiping at a stray tear. "He hasn't bothered me for some time, but now, he's back to asking me out and getting upset about being turned down."

His anger escalated like a plane taking off, making him want to get his hands on the man who continued to harass and frighten Hannah. Inside he seethed, but with a Herculean effort, he managed to remain calm on the outside.

"Don't cry," he murmured, rising to pull her up from the chair and into his arms.

With both arms around her waist, he tucked his head in beside hers, content to just hold her close. At first, she froze, her body stiff and unyielding as a board. Gradually, when he remained still—not pushing her for any reaction—she melted against him, her arms sliding up his chest to encircle his neck. The sobs were soft, like a kitten mewing. He held on as her tears tamed his avenger spirit like water on a fire. There would be another day—and he'd be ready.

They stood for several minutes, swaying slightly. When she lifted her head, he blinked several times, and pulled farther back, forcing himself to lower tense shoulders and relax his arms to his sides.

With concentration, he managed to control the tone of his voice, keeping it low and even. "Are you okay?"

Hannah nodded, stepped around him, and after hesitating a moment, sat down and reached for her coffee cup. After a quick sip, she returned it to the saucer and then arranged it in perfect alignment with his.

His scowl returned. "I can tell the guy to get lost."

"No, there's no need," she said, her gaze jerking up to meet his. "He's nothing."

For John, the man was far from being "nothing." Sooner or later, the guy would return—and he'd take care of the situation, with or without her permission.

****

Hannah was almost sorry she'd invited John over for coffee earlier in the morning. Sure, she liked him—a lot—but the feelings she was beginning to have for him were unlike anything she'd ever felt for a man before. There had also been a moment when she'd looked up into his blazing eyes and felt fear. But then his tender side had returned. He was an odd mixture of conquering hero and gentle protector. Lion and teddy bear. She trusted him. A knight in shining armor who would ride to her defense if necessary.

She was sorry for the topic of conversation, not for his presence.

But he had left soon after finishing the coffee, and now she was bored. The afternoon stretched out ahead of her.

With the radio playing softly, she laid the evening's outfit on the foot of the bed. A loud knocking on her apartment door had her racing across the small living room, all smiles, hoping John had returned. With a hand on the knob, she hesitated, remembering her mother had always cautioned her never to open the door without knowing who was on the other side. "Who's there?"

"Open the door, Hannah. It's Eddie."

Her heart thudded, then surged. "No. I'll see you next week at work."

"Open it. *Now*."

His demand was accompanied by more pounding. No way would she allow him another opportunity to push into her home.

"Hey, buddy. What's the problem?" John's muffled voice came through the door.

Never had she had a prayer answered before she even asked.

"This is none of your business."

"It's definitely my business if you're harassing Hannah. She's not interested in your attention, so leave. Now."

He was standing up for her. Hannah hovered by the door with a trembling hand resting near her throat, above her thundering heart.

"This is between Hannah and me. Get lost."

She could hear a scuffle, then some obscenities being hurled at John, and finally, the front door of the boarding house slamming a floor below her.

With caution, she unlocked her door and peeked out. John trotted back up the stairs, calling out to unseen others that everything was okay now. That's when she noticed the two other second-floor residents standing out in the hall, staring toward the stairs. The incident had caught the attention of everyone in the house.

Her heart sank. If word got back to the owner, she might lose her job collecting rents and then either have to start paying rent, which she couldn't afford, or move.

At the top of the stairs, he turned toward her, not

hesitating a step as he brushed past her into her apartment. "We need to talk," he informed when he stopped inside and turned back to face her.

She hesitated only a moment before joining him inside and closing the door. Her heartbeat was still erratic when she faced him. Anger had transformed his gaze from calm to stormy, but she didn't fear this man who had just intervened to protect her. "Thank you."

"There needs to be a change of policy here."

Hannah waited, her fingers clenched and shoulders tense.

"Starting immediately, the front door of the boardinghouse will be locked—day and night. Each resident has a key, right?" When she only nodded, he continued, "Good. Tomorrow—or better yet, right now—go door-to-door and tell everyone that from now on, they will need to use their key to come in the front and back doors. They will remain locked to keep the riffraff outside. Agreed?"

She nodded. That was actually a good idea. "I'll tell everyone now." She turned toward the door, feeling his presence right behind her. When a hand slid along her upper arm, she stopped and turned to step into his waiting arms. "Thank you," she mumbled again against his chest.

His body provided needed warmth and security. She hardly knew him, yet trusted him explicitly. What was it about John that made her instantly believe him and do whatever he said? The answer was easy. Everything about him screamed honesty and integrity.

"Come on, let's tell everyone before…"

She stood staring up into his eyes, wondering what he'd stopped himself from saying. When he shook his head and pivoted to leave the apartment, she followed. Gratitude welled up inside, choking her with a desire to cry. After his heroic gesture of ushering Eddie away from her door, she owed him so much more than a hot meal each night.

After making the rounds, he escorted her back to her door. "Um, I…um…" She had a difficult time maintaining eye contact. Why couldn't she just tell him how much she'd grown to care about him and how much he meant to her? When he reached a finger out and used it to lift her chin, she slowly raised her gaze to meet his.

"You can tell me anything, pretty lady." When she only stared up into his eyes, he continued. "Yes, I was angry earlier and a bit physical with the guy, but I think he understands not to come here again and not to bother you at work. I need you to let me know if he doesn't do as he promised me he would."

His voice was calm, yet held a cold hardness that had her convinced he was capable of handling the situation if Eddie chose to go back on his word. She felt guilty, as if naming him as her boyfriend had dragged him into this mess. She had to be sure he wasn't upset with her lying to Eddie about her relationship with him but hesitated.

"What's on your mind?"

She started to lower her head, but his hand under her chin refused it permission to bow. She glanced around, wondering if the neighbors were listening just inside their doors. "Can you come back inside for a few minutes?"

He nodded, following without a word when she entered her apartment and moved into the living room to perch on the sofa's edge. "Thank you for being so sweet and riding to my rescue. Despite telling him about you a couple of days ago, he insisted on taking me out again. I turned him down. He's…persistent."

"What's his full name again?"

"What? Oh, it's Stone. Eddie Stone."

"If he's ever stupid enough to bother you again, be sure to remind him that your guy lives right across the hall."

My guy? Oh how she was starting to wish that were true.

"I dread going to work next week." She shoved her hands into the hair on each side of her head, lifting the heavy thickness off her neck. She held it taunt for a moment before removing her hands and allowing the strands to flop back to their former place.

"I don't think he'll bother you again."

His tone caught her attention, causing her to narrow her eyes, and draw her brows in a bit closer. "What did you say to him?"

"It doesn't matter." John reached out and gently cupped both her upper arms, tugging slightly until she stood close. Then he leaned in and kissed her on the forehead. "Don't worry about him—and don't feel guilty about what you said to him. In fact, besides going to Hughes' dinner party tonight," he drawled, leaning back to smile down at her upturned face, "why don't we go out together sometime soon…and then it'll be the truth?"

Yes, yes, yes. "I'd enjoy that. Thank you."

"Okay, great. I'll see you later."

His arms dropped to his side, yet he hesitated a moment—a moment while she prayed he'd kiss her goodbye, but he only smiled again and then walked out the door.

Disappointment sent a tingle down to her toes, but she wasn't one to give up on a dream.

He was her white knight—ready to defend her honor. She'd only needed someone to stand up for her once before today, but she definitely appreciated what he'd done. Having John live close would help her sleep at night.

"Mother," she said, glancing toward the ceiling, "I wish you could be here to meet John. You'd love him, too."

From the first day—from the moment he stood in front of her holding out a bouquet of spaghetti, her heart had belonged to him—whether he wanted it or not. Now, her future held excitement and promise.

Chapter Eight

With more control than he would have thought possible, John closed and locked his apartment door when he really wanted to slam it with every ounce of strength he possessed. He headed for the kitchen for a drink of water. Thankfully, the techniques he'd been taught as a kid actually worked. Once he'd grabbed Eddie's arm and tucked it up behind him while holding the man's thumb bent at an angle, walking him out the front door of the boardinghouse had been easy. The man blustered a lot about his rights to visit Hannah if he wanted, but the higher his arm was raised, the less he protested.

He had wanted to hit the guy for upsetting Hannah, but violence wasn't part of his nature. Until now. He knew whatever measures had been needed to protect her today would have been used—and would be used again in the future—if necessary. She was becoming important.

"Who am I kidding? She's been important ever since I met her."

The heart thump he'd felt when she admitted telling the other man they were a couple had been an unusual experience, but the instant transformation from shock to chest-swelling pride surprised him more than anything else.

He hadn't counted on falling for Vince's daughter.

The thought of another man sniffing around Hannah sent irritation shooting through his system like a car around a race track. Eddie Stone had riled him.

The longer he pondered, the more sure he was that Vince should be notified. Of course, he couldn't chance Hannah overhearing his conversation, so going to the corner market was mandatory. Without wasting another moment, he strode out the door.

The afternoon was warm with a slight breeze, meaning lots of folks were out walking and kids were playing in the small yards.

"Good afternoon," the clerk called out when John entered.

"Hi. Can I use the phone?"

"Sure. The booth's in the back near the canned goods display."

"Thanks."

At the back of the market, he stepped inside the small enclosure and closed the red painted door behind him. Again, he initiated the process that finally connected him with the compound.

"Hello?"

He couldn't believe the don had answered his own phone. That almost never happened. "Hi, it's John."

"Hey, boy. Good to hear from you. How's it going with your new job?"

"Going good. My team is designing a new wing for one of his planes. I'm learning and contributing."

"Good. Good. How's the other reason for you being out there?"

"I'm glad you brought that up since that's why I'm calling. I'd like you to check on someone for me." He hesitated, scowling as he pictured the way he'd tossed the guy out onto the sidewalk. He never expected to see him again, but a prudent man always investigated his enemy. "Eddie Stone. He works where she does."

"A problem?"

"No, just an annoyance, but it upsets her."

"Will do. Give me a little time."

"And remember, I'm asking that you *check out* the situation, not *remove* the situation. Understand?" he added quickly.

"Yeah, yeah. I got ears, boy."

The static grew stronger for a moment, then subsided. "So, how's everything else?"

John wasn't sure what to say. Vince was fishing, but for what?

"What do you mean?"

"I'm just wondering what you think of your landlady?"

"She's lovely." The words popped out without forethought, but now he calculated each one. "Smart and kind—and really cares about the elderly tenants."

"What did Sadie tell her about her father?"

John hesitated. This wouldn't make the old man happy, but he hesitated to add to his lies—or withheld truths. This truth would just have to hurt. "She gave her daughter a father a little girl could look up to."

"What do you mean?"

"A policeman, killed in the line of duty."

Silence.

"Still there?"

"Yeah. Guess I can't blame her. It's just ironic." A heavy sigh whispered through the line.

"Well, I've got to go," John finally said.

"Goodbye, boy. I'll call if there's anything urgent

you should know."

He hung up but stood staring at the phone as if waiting for it to ring. Every way he turned, people weren't happy. He felt guilty for being the messenger of bad news, but Vince had made his choices. The original decisions might have been made with the best intentions, but if the man didn't like the outcome, at least the results were of his own making.

John left the store, taking a long loop around several blocks on the way back to the boardinghouse. It allowed time to ponder the mess he'd gotten himself into. When he agreed to watch out for Hannah, he never expected to start caring about her. Now, he was lying to her left and right. He momentarily closed his eyes, shaking his head. Well, not outright, but lying by withholding the truth. How could he have been so stupid? And he couldn't even talk the situation over with his mother. The first words out of her mouth would be, *"I told you so."*

John kept walking but glanced toward the heavens. Would there be help coming from above for someone who willfully lied?

He ducked under a low-hanging limb that stretched across part of the sidewalk. Straightening, he rubbed his chest, trying to ease the burning. The turmoil was giving him indigestion, yet the one-sided debate continued. What if he told her the truth, admitting his part in the deception? That thought slowed his steps. What would happen? He turned right, heading for the park bench partially hidden in a cluster of trees.

She might hate me for ruining the heroic image she has of her father.

That was always a possibility, but more

importantly, it would shatter the image of her recently deceased mother. How could he do that to her?

He sat on the seat within the cool shade. The choices were limited. Ruin the memories of her mother and the larger-than-life father, or leave her in the dark about the past, sad but content. But what if she found out about Vince sometime in the future and subsequently realized how John had been lying to her ever since he'd moved in?

The groan slipped out into the warm afternoon. He was doomed whichever way he chose to handle the situation.

"I'm clearly behind the eight ball on this one," he muttered, scratching his cheek.

Either way—continue the lie or confess everything he knew—he'd lose in the end.

John closed his eyes, brows drawn together. That was something he'd have to face at another time. Right now, he had just over an hour until the car would arrive to take them to the party.

What other excitement did the evening hold?

****

Ten minutes before six, John stood at Hannah's door and knocked. After half-an-hour of self-lecture on setting aside things he couldn't do anything about and concentrating on having a good time, he was actually looking forward to the evening.

The door opened, and his jaw went slack. His heart thudded, and he blinked several times before opening his mouth, but no words came out.

"Are you okay?" She leaned forward a few inches and reached out a hand toward him.

He cleared his throat, allowing a soft chuckle to

slip out into the quietness of the empty hall. "I'm stunned." He took her hand. "You are beautiful. I'll be the envy of every man there."

Her face flushed as she lowered her chin and smiled.

"Are you ready?"

"Yes," she said, holding up a small clutch purse. "Am I dressed right for tonight's affair?"

"You're perfect." He tucked her hand in the crook of his arm and pulled the door closed behind them. "I thought we'd wait downstairs for the car. It should be along in a minute or two."

At the top of the stairs, he hesitated, allowing her a moment to put a hand on the railing and prepare to descend the steps in the high-heeled shoes. The dress glistened when she moved, drawing his eyes to the draped front and slinky, blue material that fit like a second skin to just below the thighs before it flared out at the bottom to almost brush the floor. With her hair swept up into a swirl and held in place with a long, black clip, the earrings emphasized her long neck, drawing his gaze and focusing his desire on kissing the smooth skin just below her jaw.

His heart thundered when she glanced toward him, blushed, and then glanced away. She was the most beautiful woman he knew.

"John, you're embarrassing me," she whispered.

"Sorry, but you take my breath away."

He put out his arm, not moving until she had slipped her arm through his, then started slowly down, allowing her to set the pace. They waited near the front door where they could see the street.

When the car drove up, he escorted her down the

front steps, helped her into the waiting vehicle, and then joined her, allowing the driver to close the car door and cocoon them in the luxury of deep, leather seats.

They were soon on the way, but John remained on his side, maintaining space between them, as if a line had been drawn down the middle of the seat. Why did he suddenly feel hesitant about holding her hand? Sure, she was Vince's daughter, but he liked her—a lot.

She stared out the window, while he silently watched her hands fidget with the small purse, opening the clasp and snapping it closed repeatedly.

"Are you nervous?"

She swiveled her head to face him. "Oh, no," she answered quickly, then took a deep breath that whispered out in a sigh. "Well, maybe a little. I'm around stars all the time, but I've never partied with them, and certainly never anyone of Mr. Hughes' status."

He pushed away concerns about her parentage and reached to take one of her hands, giving it a little squeeze. "Try to remember he's just a man."

"A very *rich* man—and a very *famous* man after his recent flight across the country."

He chuckled, bringing her hand up to kiss each finger. "Thank you for coming with me tonight. The evening should prove to be very interesting."

They rode the rest of the way in silence until the car turned onto the driveway leading up to the Beverly Hills Hotel.

"Oh, John, look at this place. It's lovely. I can't wait to see the inside. Very impressive. Look at the red tiled roof and the porte cochere."

"The what?"

She turned to glance at him. "The porte cochere? It's an awning that extends out from the building so cars can pull up and let off passengers without them getting wet. They're very popular with the movie stars at the studio where I work. They all want one added to their homes."

He shrugged. "There aren't porte—whatevers—in Mobile," he said, adding a chuckle.

She smiled, but her attention had already focused back on the surroundings. When the car stopped, a young man stepped forward to open the door.

Unlike Hannah, John's attention hadn't been on the multi-storied building, but all the late-model cars lining the driveway—every one of them able to make him drool and wish to someday own one.

"Good evening, sir. May I escort you and the lady to your party?" The young man bowed slightly as he shut the car door behind them.

"The Hughes' party?"

"Ah, yes sir. Right this way," he instructed, leading them through an arched entryway and holding open the main door.

They crossed the marble floor, her heels clicking a cadence that drew his attention. Her profile intrigued him. A creamy complexion set against chestnut brown hair and large, dark blue eyes, demure and graceful—a lady from her head to her polished toenails. Tonight, she looked breathtaking enough to give any one of Paramount's leading ladies reason to be jealous.

Even as pride swelled his chest at her being his date, he watched her gaze travel from right to left and then up toward the magnificent elevated ceiling. Sure, the building was beautiful with its Mediterranean architecture and furnishings, but it didn't hold a candle to the stunning beauty digging her fingers into his arm as they made their entrance.

Howard Hughes was tall, several inches above most of the men, making him easily recognizable when they were shown into the ballroom. Familiar faces from the silver screen, as well as numerous others, mingled in a close orbit, but Mae West and Claudette Colbert currently held his focus.

Beside him, Hannah cleared her throat, drawing his attention. She leaned close and lowered her voice. "John, do you know anyone?"

"Only a couple, but come on, and I'll introduce you to Mr. Hughes."

She remained at his side when he moved forward, but her silence spoke volumes. He took her hand from the crook of his arm and linked their fingers, giving her a reassuring squeeze that drew her gaze. After a quick wink, he focused on his objective and moved forward.

Like Mr. Hughes, all the men wore suits, but some had chosen to dress more casual and not wear ties. John felt right at home with the wide lapels and crisp pleated slacks of his navy graduation suit—another gift from Vince that his mother didn't need to learn about.

"Ah, John, I'm glad you could come." His boss shook his extended hand and then turned toward Hannah. "And who is your date for this evening?"

"Mr. Hughes, this is Hannah Montgomery."

He turned his full attention on her, reaching out to take her hand. "It's my pleasure to meet you, Miss Montgomery."

John watched, silent but seething, while Howard Hughes slowly smiled, then skimmed her body with a dark gaze that ignited an inner urge to protect what was his. With one hand clenched at his side, he instinctively stepped forward and partially inserted himself between the two, requiring the other man to release Hannah's hand.

"If you'll excuse us," he said, glancing between Mr. Hughes and Hannah before pinning the other man with a pointed gaze. "We're on our way to get a drink before I introduce her around to your other guests."

"Sure. And welcome." One brow rose as he grinned. "By the way, how's Vince doing?"

He clamped his jaws together to keep from showing his utter shock. Was this his boss' subtle way of putting him in his place for being possessive about Hannah? Maybe. Vince had mentioned the man owed him a favor—*had* he called in that favor with a request that his stepson be hired, and subsequently included in the prestigious project...because of Vince? Had Vince lied to him?

"Fine," he managed to get out. "At least the last time I saw him."

His boss nodded. "Give him my best next time you talk with him."

The man turned back to the tight group surrounding him and the skimpily dressed woman hanging on his arm.

John now wondered if he should have even come to the party. He had nothing in common with movie stars and directors. He'd rather be at home having dinner *alone* with Hannah.

Her sigh drew his attention. He turned and gave her a tight smile. "I'm sorry." He spoke low for their ears only while angling them away from the crowd huddled around the great man and focusing on those standing near the buffet table. "I know he has a reputation with the ladies, but I'm a little surprised he'd give you the once-over with me standing right there."

She smiled and lowered her chin with a soft laugh. "Don't worry about it. It's not important. I'm surprised he even glanced my way."

"He likes beautiful women, and that definitely includes you," he couldn't help but murmur near her ear. When she flushed, he relaxed.

"So, he knows Vince?"

The question came as a surprise, but as they say, the world was getting smaller. "Guess so. Come on, let's get something to drink, and I'll introduce you to a couple of my coworkers. Actually, they're the only other ones I know here," he added with a soft chuckle.

With his hand barely touching her lower back, he ushered her through the crowd toward a small group of men and women standing near the sidelines. The room glistened with lights reflecting a rainbow of colors off beautiful gowns, but none of the starlets or society women paying homage to Mr. Hughes could hold a candle to his Hannah. With a grace and regal bearing of someone raised in society instead of the working class community she hailed from, she met each person with a demure but friendly smile, instantly putting them at ease in her company.

His chest swelled. Hannah was stunning...and she was with *him*.

****

Hannah had been standing for almost two hours, sipping a watered-down cola and wishing the evening would end. The shoes that had fit her mother so well

115

pinched her feet, leaving them numb and throbbing.

When John leaned over to whisper in her ear, she tried to smile without grimacing.

"Are you about ready to go home?"

Her shoulders sagged, her weary body ready to weep with gratitude. A nod and a weak grin from her were all it took for him to take action. She'd really liked two of the ladies she'd met, but the rest were superficial, talking about themselves and their success, or the success of their husbands, until she wanted to scream.

"Come on. Let's thank our host."

Mr. Hughes smiled as they approached. "Leaving?" When John nodded, he continued, "Glad you could come. I'll see you Monday."

"Thank you for a lovely evening, sir." Her polite comment drew Mr. Hughes' attention, making her wish she had kept her mouth shut.

He gazed straight into her eyes, nodded his head a fraction, and then smiled just enough to barely move his lips. His mannerisms reminded her of directors telling the actors to smirk as if they know something that the other person doesn't. She shivered. He wasn't at all how she thought he'd be. How could John work with this man? He gave her chills down her back.

"Thanks for inviting us." John's words drew the man's gaze off her and back to himself.

Hannah released a held breath when he took her arm and led the way from the room, through the expansive lobby, and out into the warm, summer evening.

While they waited for the car to pull up, he took several deep breaths himself. "I much prefer the smell of trees and flowers out here to the stale cigarette smoke we had to endure inside."

"I agree. The odor was beginning to give me a headache," she admitted, then stopped and lowered her chin, looking up at him from beneath dark lashes. "Sorry, I shouldn't have said that." She didn't want him to think she hadn't enjoyed their night together.

"Why not? I agree. That room was too warm and stuffy. I'm glad to be outside—and alone with you."

He leaned over and kissed her cheek just as the car pulled up and the driver got out to come around and open the car door for them. The heat warming her neck and cheeks had nothing to do with the warm summer evening and everything to do with John's public display of affection. On one hand, she was a little embarrassed, yet inside, her stomach was in knots while pride overruled discomfort at the thought of him not caring who saw them together.

Her first party with the upper crust of society and other than the beautiful dresses, the magnificent hotel, and excited butterflies from John's kiss, she couldn't think of much else to put in her diary when she got home. Sure, she'd met the infamous Howard Hughes, but she'd been disappointed—he'd invited some of his staff, but never left the circle of Hollywood and business elites.

In the car, she leaned her head back against the seat, closed her eyes, and allowed herself to drift along with the rhythm of the moving car.

"Hey, Sleeping Beauty."

The whispered words were followed by a light brush of lips on her forehead. She woke slowly, smiling, blinking several times while she remained a captive of John's intense gaze. Seconds ticked by while her fuzzy mind struggled to focus. Though reluctant to leave the dream of being held in his arms, she found wakeful reality flooded her mind, leaving her heated body throbbing long after he came around to her side of the car, took her hand, and assisted her from the vehicle.

Usually, young men left her on the porch when a date ended, but tonight was different. It felt a bit awkward when he unlocked the front door and ushered her inside the boarding house then followed her upstairs. She couldn't help but imagine them coming home together after an evening out and entering their apartment as a couple.

The thought sent a shiver down her arms.

"Are you cold?"

"No." Still, it felt good when his warm hand held hers until they arrived at her door.

"Thank you for inviting me to join you tonight. I enjoyed it." She pulled out her key, then hesitated.

Will he kiss me?

"You were the most beautiful woman there."

Gentle fingers slid along her jaw, tilting her head back. In slow increments, she raised her gaze from his shirt collar to his Adam's apple, then on up to meet his intense stare. Without a word and with the barest touch, he held her captive as he leaned forward to run the rough pad of a thumb along her jaw just before he momentarily hovered, then brushed his lips across hers.

No words were necessary. She leaned into his warmth, sliding a hand up his chest underneath the edge of his suit jacket, blazing a trail that ended when her fingertips touched his neck just above his shirt collar.

His arms slid around to embrace and cuddle her closer. Pressed against him, her body demanded more—but sanity forced its way past desire. She pulled back, instantly regretting the decision, but knowing it was the right thing to do. Her mother's words filled her head. *Men will respect you, but only if you first respect yourself.*

"I'm sorry, Hannah. I, um, well…"

She sagged in relief, unable to stop a smile from spreading at the thought of this take-charge, in-control guy being flustered, too. "We'd better call it a night. You're leaving early in the morning for Alabama, right?"

A heavy sigh whispered into the cool air of the hallway. "Yes," he admitted, stepping back and allowing his arms to relax to his sides. "I'll be back late Wednesday night, so are we on for supper Thursday?"

His boyish smile drew her like flowers to the sun. "Absolutely. See you then."

He raised a hand, as if to touch one last time, but lowered it. "Good night."

Hannah turned, unlocked her door, and stepped inside, closing it without watching him walk to his apartment. She leaned back against the wooden door and shut her eyes while reliving his kiss. A smile lurked as she considered how the past few minutes would fill her diary page that night, but it was thoughts of the future—a future that now appeared to include John— that she knew would keep her awake late into the night.

Since John moved in, each day brought something new into her life. She almost giggled as she pushed away from the door and headed toward her bedroom. What was in store for her tomorrow?

Chapter Nine

The plane flight was long and tiring, not to mention bumpy. John ate right before boarding, which ended up being a mistake. Even now, as he stood to exit the plane, he rested a hand over his stomach. A few minutes later, the intense, Alabama heat slammed into his face, tightened every muscle in his body, and churned his stomach like a witch stirring her brew.

Once outside the plane, he hesitated a moment at the top of the metal stairs to breathe in the humidity-laden air. Across the tarmac, his mother stood waving, a smile stretched across her face as if he'd been gone a year instead of a couple of months.

Upon reaching the bottom of the stairs, his stride ate up the distance between them. "Hi, Mom."

He wrapped an arm around her shoulders and hugged. She smelled of vanilla and Ivory soap. It never failed to surprise him what could bring back memories. He smiled down into her upturned face, but guilt overshadowed the moment. He owed her so much.

"You look good, son."

He chuckled. "What did you expect? I've only been gone for the summer."

John chose to remain silent while they made their way through the airport, navigating around slower-moving people. Giant ceiling fans disturbed the air, making it tolerable, but once outside, the sweltering heat of late summer was still enough to wilt flowers. The humidity had sweat running down his sides under his loose-fitting, blue shirt, but at least the heat was only in the mid-eighties versus nineties or above.

The drive home in his grandfather's old Ford was a little better, but he knew his mother was only biding her time. She rarely talked when she drove, choosing to concentrate on the road and other cars, but soon, she'd start with the questions, and he'd tell her the truth. His mother would be disappointed about his involvement with Vince and Hannah, but hopefully she'd understand. With luck, she might even help with suggestions on how to tell Hannah about her father— once she stopped yelling about him agreeing to help Vince.

He rolled his eyes and counted the miles to their small, wood-sided home. There were still patches of green, but things looked drier this year—signs of excessive heat and limited rain. Nothing new.

The neighborhood hadn't changed much in the years he'd lived in Mobile. People moved into town and others left, but most folks, like his grandparents and probably his mother, lived in the same house until they made their final journey at death.

"Here we are, and I have a nice pitcher of tea waiting in the icebox."

"Great."

At the door, he allowed his mother to enter first and took a moment to toss the satchel on his bed before joining her in the kitchen.

"Have a seat. It's probably cooler in here since the sun is setting on the other side of the house."

He drank deep, letting the cool liquid relieve his

parched throat. With the chair slid back slightly and both arms resting on the table, he wrapped his hands around the cool glass and stared at the few chunks of ice floating in the sweet drink.

"Son, something's been on your mind since you landed. Want to share it?"

She sat across from him, a frown wiping away the pleasant smile she had sported since leaving the airport.

"Yes, but you're not going to be happy, so I'm going to ask that you not voice your opinion—I already know it—and just help me come up with a solution."

Her frown deepened, but he knew she'd listen, tell him what she thought—hopefully with less ranting than usual—and then she'd try to help.

"You warned me about Vince—and you were right—but not about what he wanted."

"He didn't want you to join his family business?"

The frown had changed slightly. She now looked leery of his next admission, and he couldn't blame her.

"No. He said I didn't have the temperament for that line of work."

"Well, amen. I raised you better than that," she said, reaching out to run a warm hand down his arm.

His stomach clenched. Her words rubbed salt in an already raw wound. He'd let her down by agreeing to Vince's request. Her faith in him would be shaken.

"Don't put anyone on a pedestal yet, Mother."

Her face relaxed, all expression gone as she lifted her chin and waited.

"When I went to New York, he asked me where I planned to apply for work, and I mentioned Howard Hughes Aviation. He offered to put in a good word, but I turned him down," he added quickly. "Then he offered to at least help me get a room at a boardinghouse. I felt the suggestion was harmless, so I agreed. Only then did he mention that his daughter manages the place and…"

"He knows where his child is living?" Her eyes widened and brows rose, but just as quickly, she wiped all expression from her face and waited.

"Yes. It's a long story that I can tell you later, but since I'd agreed to let him get me a room, he asked if I'd be willing to keep an eye on her, and let him know if she needed anything."

"He asked you to spy on her?"

The narrowed gaze followed closely by pursed lips quirked up on one corner told him how his mother felt about the entire situation. He didn't blame her, but, hopefully, she'd keep an open mind. This wasn't the time for a tirade.

He breathed in slowly, held it for a couple moments, then quietly released it before continuing. "Technically, but not like you probably think. He asked me to let him know if, for instance, she lost her job and couldn't afford food. That kind of thing. I don't report weekly on her comings and goings or anything like that."

"Is that why you offered to pay for food and she cooks for you?"

"No," he answered, chuckling. "That was self-preservation." He was encouraged to see her smile and nod. "But agreeing to let him know if she got into dire straits has backfired."

"How's that?" She was frowning again, but this time with curiosity, not anger.

John sent a silent thank you winging heavenward.

"One night over dinner, she told me about her mother and father."

"She knows about Vince?"

"No. Her mother gave her a fantasy father. A policeman who died a hero."

"Oh my." She pulled the hankie from her dress pocket and wiped perspiration from her face.

"For over a month, I've known the truth, yet not told her. And to complicate things," he stated, glancing down at his hands before lifting his gaze to connect with his mother's, "I think I'm in love with Hannah."

"Goodness. That makes this more difficult, doesn't it?" She lifted the glass and took a swallow. "If you tell her the truth, she'll think you've been intentionally lying to her all this time."

"True, but worse than that, I'll be making her deceased mother a liar. She idolizes the lady." Just the thought of causing her that kind of pain made his stomach churn. How had he ever let himself get into such a mess?

"Oh, I hadn't thought about that. So, what are you going to do? You have to tell her."

"I agree." He ran fingers up through his hair before releasing a deep sigh. "I do have to tell her, but as the saying goes, no one loves the bearer of bad news."

She shrugged. "True. So, like I asked before, what do you plan to do?"

"If I didn't care, I could just tell her and let the chips fall where they fall, but that's not the case." He ran his hand along his tea glass, watching the condensation trickle down the side to puddle on the table while he fought to find the words. He raised his gaze and looked toward his mother. "I don't know what to do. Is there a better place or time to pull the rug out from under her feet when I explain how her life has been filled with one lie after the other?" He sucked in a deep breath and released it slowly. His next words were spoken softly. "Is there ever a good way to break a girl's heart?"

His mother sat staring at him for long, silent moments before she spoke. "Son, this isn't my decision to make, but you know I didn't raise you to lie to people—especially people you care about. I'd suggest that you tell her the truth right away and apologize for your part in the scheme."

"But I'm not part of anything," he pleaded.

She only raised her eyebrows, remaining silent.

"Okay. *Technically*, I'm a part of it, but, believe me, I'll never report on her unless her life is in danger."

"Then tell her that part also."

He nodded, knowing she was right.

I just need to find the right time to tell Hannah the whole story.

"How did I ever get into this mess? I've never wanted anything from Vince."

"Except money for an education."

Her words slammed into him like a slap to the face. True, he'd needed the money to have had any chance of achieving his life's goal of designing planes, but at that time, it never dawned on him the man might someday ask for anything in return.

He forced his face to remain neutral, hiding his inner turmoil while he watched his mother process their discussion.

Finally, she blinked several times, sighed, and shrugged, a sad grin transforming her face. "I'm sorry," she said, reaching across to touch his arm. "That was rude. There was no reason for you to refuse his offer. He owed you that much, but in the future, please be more cautious. That's all I'm saying. He *was* always very fond of you."

His relief was palatable. Her anticipated ranting about Vince was quailed by concern for him and Hannah.

He squeezed her hand, leaning forward until he looked directly into her eyes. "Trust me, I've learned my lesson. I'll never agree to do another 'little favor,' as he put it."

She hesitated, but when he didn't move or speak, she finally nodded. "Okay. You've left the nest, and although it seems that truth has boarded one of your planes and taken flight, I trust you to straighten this situation out and make things right."

"Thank you." He squeezed her hand, then released it. "So, how about filling me in on Vince's history. Maybe it will help me when I explain things to Hannah."

She looked more resigned than happy, but she nodded and relaxed back in her chair. He could almost hear the wheels turning in her brain while she ran a finger around the rim of her glass, like a race car traveling slowly around a circular track. She, no doubt, was trying to decide how much to tell him, and what he didn't need to know. A frown flashed but was quickly erased in an attempt to hide his irritation at the thought of her holding back possible important facts.

"What exactly do you want to know?"

"Why don't you start at the beginning—or at least as far back as you know."

Her gaze dropped to a point in the middle of his chest, even though he could tell her mind was a million miles away—or maybe only fifteen hundred miles north. He sat quietly, patiently waiting for her to start. He had learned the ability to remain calm and silent while he weighed facts and considered alternatives. Although it had started out as a way to keep from sassing his mother and thus staying out of trouble, he learned over the years that it worked well when he wanted something the other person was reluctant to give. He simply outwaited them. Once the silence became uncomfortable, they usually gave in. It was a harmless strategy that had worked before—and was working today.

She finally lifted her gaze to connect with his, her stare direct, but her voice cautious. "You were about nine, and I was working nights at a café here in Mobile. One Thursday evening, Vince and two men came in for coffee."

A gentle smile softened her mouth and eased the tension around her eyes. It also confirmed what he remembered from his childhood, but what he now knew was love. His mother had loved Vince with a passion.

"By the time they left, I had a date with him for the next night, and within three months, we were married." A slight smile softened her face. "He loved you from the moment he met you. He called you his 'Little Man.' " Her features suddenly grew hard. "But you weren't his son, and I refused to allow him to take you around his men. I didn't want you mixed up in all that mess."

"You mean the mafia?"

She hesitated for only a moment before she

nodded. "I didn't understand at first what he did for a living. There weren't too many gangsters coming in for coffee down here in Alabama. Know what I mean?" When he nodded, she continued, "By the time I realized what he was involved in, we were already married, and I loved him enough to stay. Well, at least as long as he kept you and I out of his racket. I didn't want you to someday have to watch over your shoulder and never know when a bullet might have your name on it."

John was pretty sure of the answer, but he had to ask. "I remember him taking me out to lunch when I turned twelve. There were a couple other men there. They were his bodyguards, if I remember correctly. Is that why we left a few days later?"

She closed her eyes and nodded. "Yes." When she opened them, her voice lowered to almost a whisper. "I still loved him, but I loved *you* more."

The heaviness in his chest was unexpected. His mother never spoke about Vince, but her admission explained the nights he heard her crying after the lights were turned off. He reached over and placed a hand on her arm, squeezed gently, and then waited. His chest barely moved as he forced his breathing to remain shallow, but there was no stopping the blood that pounded in his ears. After years of wondering, would the truth set him free, or would he regret knowing?

She sucked in a deep breath and allowed it to escape in a loud huff. "I was young and head-over-heels in love." Instantly, her face closed in, eyes glaring and lips compressed. "Love," she spat. The single word resonated like an oath, forced through gritted teeth. Just as quickly, the tension was gone and her face relaxed. "Sorry," she whispered, a shrug easing her shoulders.

"Take your time." Guilt at putting his mother through this turmoil almost had him stopping the discussion, but maybe getting her to talk about the past might mean he could share her load, ease her concerns, and eliminate some of her stress.

She nodded, turning her tea glass in circles within her hands. "At first, I thought he headed an import-export company. He kept the truth from me for almost two months. Talk about naïve." A sheepish grin rested on her face for a moment before it disappeared. "You had started school up there, and I didn't know what to do. He had a nice home and cars, and he bought me presents. I'd never had anyone—a man—buy me presents. And he spoiled you. You were so happy when he came home each evening."

When a shroud of silence fell, he sipped his tepid tea and waited. His patience paid off.

"Then, just before you turned twelve, you started to ask questions. Seems kids at school were talking, and you came home wanting to know if Vince, the man who took you on picnics and went to all your baseball games, was a mafia boss and killed people."

He nodded. "I remember that happening a few days before he took me to lunch for my birthday."

"That was the final straw. I bought the train tickets, and we headed back south."

"I enjoyed the train ride, but as time passed, I realized we wouldn't be going back. I remember telling you—often—that I wanted to go live with Vince. I'm sorry." It was his turn to feel sheepish, but now wasn't the time to dwell on all the other hurtful things he had said to her when she refused him his heart's desire.

"That was a long time ago." She reached out to

brush a hand softly across his.

Her smile reminded him of the statue of Mary at the church. Compassionate and forgiving.

"So, you left him because of me?" He hadn't seen her as unselfish then. No, he'd resented her—not caring how upset or angry she got when he talked incessantly about Vince or recited the man's virtues and threw all his support in the man's corner.

She shook her head, raising her glass and swallowing some tea before she scowled and set it back on the table. "No, not entirely. When you got home from the restaurant, you were bubbling over with everything you'd seen, including the other men. Later that night, Vince and I had a huge argument. We both said things." She hesitated, but then continued, "He let it slip that he had a daughter that he'd never seen, except in pictures. I was stunned."

"I'm surprised he didn't tell you about Hannah before you were married." Why had Vince paid so much attention to him and yet not cared enough about his own daughter to even visit her? He wasn't sure what to make of the situation. "But you knew he'd been married before."

Her eyes were focused on the red-and-white checkered tablecloth while she slowly nodded. One short fingernail traced the edge of a red square, once, then again before her hand stilled and she looked up. "Yes, I knew he'd been married, but I wasn't allowed to mention his first wife."

He frowned.

But before he could speak, his mother continued, her words tumbling out in her rush to clarify her statement. "Don't get me wrong—Vince was always good to me. He never laid a hand on me in anger, but I pressed him once about her, and his temper—well, let's just say that when he told me never to mention her again, I knew to keep my questions to myself." A wry smile accompanied her shrug.

John had no desire, and certainly no need, to know any more about Vince's first wife. As a kid, he had always liked his stepfather...even loved him. Over the years, after his mother moved to Alabama, and despite coming to realize Vince was a mafia don, he had always respected the older man.

Silence weighed heavily on his shoulders.

After a minute of them both staring at their hands, his mother shook her head, as if erasing the subject from her mind, and dredged up a timid smile. "So, when do you have to leave?"

He knew she'd hate to hear the answer, but after all, this was a business trip. "Early tomorrow morning." He held his breath, waiting for her to react, but she remained calm. Her gaze held his while he counted the seconds.

With only a nod, she stood. "I'll make supper."

She left him staring after her. How could she make him feel guilty without even trying?

Chapter Ten

A slip of paper hung on John's door the day after he arrived home from Atlanta—a note instructing him to "call his friend in New York." Though he would have preferred to make the call from the market, a glance at the wall clock told him there wasn't enough time. Hannah worked hard all day and came home to make dinner for him, and a lifetime of arriving at his mother's table on time for meals had taught him not to keep her waiting.

He rubbed his forehead, closing his eyes for a moment against the growing pain. Even gently rolling his head from one side to the other then forward and back didn't ease the tight muscles of his neck and shoulders. The game had gone on long enough. Like a fish swallowing the worm only to feel the prick of the hook, he knew he stood to lose Hannah when she learned the truth. In the meantime, he needed to make this call, to be sure she was safe. Not for Vince, but for himself.

After a fugitive glance into the hall that made him think of the Street and Smith radio program, *Detective Story Hour,* he crossed to the phone and dialed the operator, going through the Los Angeles and New York operators, and then the system Vince had set up for security. He leaned his head back against the wall and waited.

"Hey, Johnny-boy. How's it going for you?"

"Fine. Just called to find out about my local friend."

"Son, you need to be more careful with picking friends," he answered, chuckling. "Just kiddin' with you, boy. Actually, the guy is clean. Stupid, maybe, but nothing else. I'd love to spend a few minutes catching up, but I've only got time to thank you for watching over—um, for doing a good job out there. Just don't get too attached." A barked laugh vibrated the line. "Now, I need to get going. I'm having dinner with a couple men that don't like being kept waiting any more than I do."

"Be careful…" He'd come close to making the potentially fatal mistake of calling Vince by name over the phone. He'd been warned that operators were paid to listen in and report certain names or callers. The last thing he wanted to do was be responsible for anything that would put Hannah in danger, or give one of the families leverage to make Vince bow.

"Sure, kid."

The line went dead, but John stared at the phone for several heartbeats before hanging it up. The situation felt out of balance. There was no way to tell for sure, but just like knowing a storm was coming, he felt sure things weren't as they seemed. Vince had been too jovial in a way that wasn't his style, and definitely too anxious to get off the phone.

Something brewed.

****

Hannah stood by the window, watching the evening wane while she wondered what life held in store. Six months ago, the future had been an exciting thing looming just around the next bend. The thought had never entered her mind that anything would turn her world upside down.

"Mama, I miss you," she whispered, laying a hand on the warm glass pane.

John had reassured her several times that he hadn't minded coming to her rescue with Eddie—in fact, he'd joked about being her avenging hero—but she felt so foolish for ever trusting the lighting technician in the first place, for agreeing to go out with him. He had a reputation, but she'd believed his words of sympathy and accepted the offered evening to "have a little fun and get your mind off your loss." If her mother hadn't recently been killed—if she hadn't felt so alone and lonely—it would never have happened.

But she might not have met John then, either.

For the past few days, he had been working on the East coast, but he'd gotten home late the previous evening—not that she had been listening for him. He'd be arriving for dinner tonight in a few minutes, and she had a special meal ready to welcome him home— meatloaf and baked potatoes staying warm in the oven. With the added treat of a couple steamed carrots, the meal would be perfect. She owed him so much.

Tonight, she wore one of her favorite dresses—in fact, the one she'd worn the day John first moved into the apartment. Was it almost two months already? Time moved fast when there was something to look forward to.

Yet lately, there had been a tension in the air that felt thick enough to cut with a knife. If only she could figure out a way to lighten the mood.

Music?

She turned on the radio, closing her eyes for a few

moments to sway to the crooning voice of Bing Crosby singing "Pennies From Heaven."

Her eyes popped open at the sound of tapping on her door. A smile widened her lips as she dashed across the room. "Who's there?"

"Someone bearing a gift."

She couldn't get the lock turned fast enough, and she opened the door to find John holding out a long-stemmed rose.

"Oh," she murmured on a soft release of breath.

"A flower for a beautiful lady." He stepped closer and kissed her cheek.

She'd never been given flowers before, let alone a rose. "John, you shouldn't have. It must have cost a fortune." She held it with reverence, not taking her gaze off the lush red bloom. "It's beautiful," she told him on a sigh. "Thank you."

She wanted to kiss him for his extravagance and thoughtfulness, but even the thought made her neck and face flush with heat. Instead, she turned toward the kitchen but had only taken one step before he had a hold on her arm and was turning her around.

No words were needed as he leaned in and tentatively brushed his lips across hers. The kiss started slow, but, like a fire bursting into flames, he pressed in and devoured, savoring. She reached her arms up around his neck to draw him closer, loving the feel of his body meshed with her own. The scent of the rose wafted down to intoxicate her as the kiss lingered and then slowly subsided.

Her thoughts floated, and her body tingling from head to foot as she slowly opened her eyes. She should say something, but no words came to mind. An inner voice told her to move, to retreat, but her heart wanted more.

When sanity returned, she drew away, allowing her arms to slide down from his shoulders until the rose was again being held between them. His intense gaze sent a shiver down her back. She swallowed, even as her stomach tightened. Was this a dream, or was it really happening?

He stepped back, taking the warmth of his body and sending another chill along her arms. His hand glided from around her waist, but his gaze continued to hold her captive while her heart pounded.

"I missed you. I saw the rose and thought of you."

She gazed up into his eyes and smiled. "I hate to say it, but I missed you also," she admitted. "I'm glad we met—that you moved in here."

A frown flickered across his face to narrow his gaze, but was quickly gone. The conversation felt stilted. What she really wanted was for him to kiss her again—and never stop. He had a way of being forceful, yet tender and considerate. It made her want to beg for more like a dog asking for another tidbit of meat.

John took a step back, cleared his throat, and grinned. "Do you have a narrow vase for the rose?"

Hannah blinked several times at the quick change of subject. "Oh, um, yes, I have a bud vase. I'll just have to cut off part of the stem." The rose deserved better than something bought at a dime-store, but her only other choice was a tea glass.

She went into the kitchen, stooping down to get the cheap, glass vase from the bottom cupboard shelf. As she filled it with water, she kept her back to him, uncertain what to say next. The mood seemed to have grown chilly in the blink of an eye.

Finally, she turned. "Did you have a tough day?"

"My day was okay. Eight hours of meetings with other engineers to share what I learned in Atlanta."

"You must be very tired. Dinner will be ready in just a minute. Why don't you take the flower and set it on the table and have a seat? I'll bring the food in."

John lingered, watching as she pulled the casserole dish from the oven. "Meatloaf. It smells wonderful. You know, it amazes me how you can work all day, standing on your feet for hours without a break, and still come home to cook a good meal. You're amazing."

She smiled with pride. "If you'll get the dish of butter from the icebox, dinner is served."

****

John sat reclining on the sofa, nursing a cup of lukewarm coffee while his stomach churned. The meal had been delicious, every bit as good as his mother's, but his efforts to stuff Vince into a neat box and forget him was proving to be more difficult than he'd thought. On the other end of the sofa, Hannah sat with an expectant gaze, as if waiting for him to respond when he hadn't even heard the question.

The wall clock ticked away the seconds.

"Are you all right?"

He glanced up from staring into his coffee cup. "Hm? Oh, sure, I'm just tired." *Liar.*

"Maybe we should call it a night and let you get some sleep," she suggested.

She leaned forward to place a gentle hand on his arm—a hand that brushed like a feather, raising fine hairs to attention where they, along with the rest of his mind, body, and soul, begged for more.

He hesitated, then nodded and stood, setting the mug on the coffee table. "I'm sorry. You made a delicious meal, and I'm—I'm just not good company tonight."

Hannah's apartment, a haven in the middle of a cold, heartless city, usually erased life's concerns, even if only for a couple of hours. Tonight, the faint but lingering aroma of their meal that wafted through the air, along with a hint of cinnamon from the sprinkle of the spice she'd warmed in a cup of water on the stove, failed to work its magic. She called her cinnamon water "adding atmosphere," but all he could think of was his mother's apple dumplings…and the conversation he'd had with her about Hannah.

He should never have come.

For a moment, he vacillated, willing to be swayed if she asked him to stay, yet knowing his mood was a sore that would continue to fester until it totally ruined the evening. Concern for Vince paced in his sub-conscience, hounding him with reminders of dark tunnels and front-page photographs.

Her frown shouted growing suspicions—suspicions that would soon generate questions. He sighed, tired of lying to her, tired of dodging questions, and tired of being the middle man who had no way to win in this situation.

This deception needed to end, but not tonight. He needed sleep, and a little time to consider how to bring up the subject. Tomorrow.

****

The trolley clanged at each intersection, warning pedestrians to be careful and keeping John awake when all he wanted to do was doze until his stop. The workday had been long, but his mind repeatedly wandered to the dilemma of how to start the conversation that would be the end of his relationship with Hannah. She'd hate him, he had no doubt, but he had no choice.

Tell her straight off or eat first and tackle it over coffee? That was a selfish question.

He glanced at the newspaper lying on the lap of the man sitting next to him. The front photograph gripped his stomach and twisted. It took every ounce of willpower not to grab the paper so he could read the story below the picture of two men lying dead in the street. The headline gave nothing away.

Could Vince be one of them?

At his stop, he stepped from the trolley car, turned left, and jogged toward the corner where a young boy was calling out for passersby to buy his papers. "Extra, extra! Read all about it! Mob families gun each other down in New York. Extra, extra!"

He slapped a nickel in the kid's hand and took the paper. After stopping a few feet away, he skimmed the story, looking for Vince's name.

Three of New York's top crime families were involved in a shootout last evening in front of Dino's Italian Restaurant that left two dead and three injured.

Vince was listed as wounded in the shoulder but doing well at the local hospital. John grunted, the sound turning the head of a woman walking by.

"Anyone with a brain knows better than that," he mumbled.

He'd watched the process in action when he was young. There had been one time when an enforcer got shot, but it wasn't life and death, so he'd been bundled into a car and brought back to the compound for treatment by the family doctor. To be left at the hospital would mean being vulnerable—readily available to whomever had just tried to kill him.

John entered the market and headed toward the back, stepping around shoppers, but not slowing down. He stopped short when he saw the phone was in use. The delay—and the uncertainty of Vince's condition—gnawed at his stomach. With the phone still in use, he read the entire article, then leaned against the wall, closed his eyes, and took time to inhale a deep breath and calm down.

The moment the man finished, John pushed away from the wall, closed himself in the small phone booth, and followed the protocol to be connected to a New York operator and through to Vince's compound. It took a couple minutes to be connected, but at least the family lieutenant confirmed the newspaper report that the older man was alive and doing well under the circumstances.

"Vince wasn't the main target, so his wounds aren't life-threatening."

The words repeated over and over in his mind. *Not life-threatening—not life threatening.*

Not this time.

He hardly remembered leaving the market or making the two-block walk home. After unlocking the front door of the boarding house, he climbed the stairs and, without conscious thought, turned toward Hannah's apartment. He rejected solitude, instead seeking reassurance that there were areas of peace and sanity—people who lived normal lives where couples sat down to dinner without ending up shot and bleeding.

Every thought, every effort was focused on getting to Hannah and holding her in his arms until his mind and body could relax. Even as he reached up to knock, he knew tonight was the night to tell her the truth. The weeks of avoidance and holding back were over.

Tonight, Hannah would learn about her *real* father.

Chapter Eleven

When Hannah heard the knock, she grabbed the match, struck it, and lit the candle sitting in the middle of the table set for two. "Perfect." The spaghetti was almost ready. There was even fresh bread, a gift from Mable Wilson in 1-D.

With a big smile, she opened the door, prepared to share the excitement of her day. Her enthusiasm dimmed when she saw the somber face.

"John, what is it?" Was his mother okay? Did he get fired? "Come in, come in." She took his hand and led him to the sofa where he remained standing, staring at her.

The chill dancing along her arms made her tremble. Was the world at war again? His face was ashen, his breathing shallow and more rapid than usual.

"Talk to me," she coaxed, taking his hands in hers and rubbing her thumbs along the chilled backs.

He slowly sucked in a deep breath. "I'm sorry. It's been a rough day, and I'm tired. Can we save the heavy discussion for later?"

His gaze held a foreboding that the lovingly orchestrated evening would not go as planned.

Hannah was no longer hungry, but she pasted on a smile. "I've made spaghetti, and we have fresh bread. I hope you like it."

"I'm sure it'll be great."

A weak smile stretched his lips, but failed to reach his eyes. She decided not to push. Before long, he'd share whatever had upset him. If he didn't, there was no way she'd allow him to go home. Her mother had once said she'd given her daughter at least a couple of her traits—dark hair and stubbornness.

Well, sometimes that's what's needed.

Hannah slid her arms up around his neck and stepped closer, drawing him into her warmth. She held him, willing to remain as long as needed.

A couple minutes passed before she felt a shiver ripple down his back.

Almost immediately, he stepped back and cleared his throat. "I'm sorry. I probably shouldn't have come tonight, but…" He turned enough to look over at the table where the candle flickered, casting a shadow against the closest wall.

"Come on. Sit down and let me serve dinner. Eating will help you feel a little better, and we can talk about what's on your mind. Sometimes sharing with someone else helps gain insight from another perspective."

His expression was guarded, tense, but he nodded, and sat down in his usual chair. She hesitated another moment before moving into the kitchen to take up their plates. Once she set them on the table, she sat down across from him.

"This smells really good. I missed lunch today."

Like every other night, John blessed the food and they ate in silence for several minutes, but Hannah's appetite was gone. She mostly moved the food in a haphazard pattern on the plate but still managed to consume a little more than John. His focus remained on his meal with little more than a token bite occasionally. She glanced several times at the clock, planning to give him fifteen minutes before she stepped in.

The minutes ticked by. Whatever was wrong, it drove his thoughts inward, leaving her alone outside his mental wall—a familiar place, but a place she refused to remain.

Enough was enough.

"Why don't I make us each a cup of coffee, and then I'll join you on the couch?"

John lifted his gaze, stared into her eyes, then nodded. While the coffee brewed, she watched him stretch out his legs where he sat, lean his head back against the sofa, then close his eyes as if intending to doze.

What in the world had him so upset, so quiet? She prayed she wouldn't have to wait long to find out. Maybe if she could get his mind off work or whatever had him in the dumpster, he'd cheer up.

Within minutes, she carried two cups to the coffee table and sat down beside him. Hope was renewed when he reached over and took her hand in his, linking their fingers. She forced her shoulders to relax as she leaned against him.

"Thank you for all the effort you went to for dinner. I wish I'd been hungrier."

"There's enough left over for another night, so you get a second chance," she said, laughing softly.

His lips lifted a fraction, but his gaze remained focused on their joined hands.

Maybe engaging him in casual conversation would help redirect his thoughts. "Did you hear about the mob shooting in New York? The paper said two men were killed and several others injured. My mother used to say they all deserved what they got, and as long as they only shot each other, the police should stay out of it and let them kill each other off."

His gaze slowly rose to meet hers, a frown marring his brow. "Is that how you feel?"

She shrugged. "I guess that opinion makes sense up to a point, but I hate all the killing. That's not how civilized people should act."

He nodded, glancing away before returning his gaze to her a moment later. "I'm sorry about not being very good company tonight. Something happened to make me realize I need to take a step back and do something I promised never to do."

Something *had* happened. She hadn't wanted to be right, but at least John was going to share it with her.

I'll be strong for him. I'll be strong.

He took a deep breath and released it slowly. "First, though, I need to give you a little history."

She nodded, but remained quiet.

"I never knew my father because he left soon after he found out my mother was expecting me. She worked two jobs and long hours, but we were doing okay. When I was about nine, mother met a man at the coffee shop where she worked, and next thing I knew, we were moving from Mobile up to New York City."

She brought her hand up to rest over her stomach. On the heels of the newspaper article and combined with the level of John's turmoil, this didn't bode well for a happy ending.

"We lived in New York for a few good years, and then my mother suddenly packed up and moved me back to Mobile. She refused to discuss my stepfather after that, but when I graduated high school, I got a letter from him offering to pay my way through college."

"That was very nice of him."

"My mother didn't think so. She didn't want me to have anything to do with him."

"Well, that's not unusual in divorces, right?"

He stared at her a moment before shrugging. "I guess so. I don't have a lot of experience in that area. Anyway, I heard almost nothing from him for four years, but each year, the tuition was paid. Then when I graduated, I got a telegram saying that he'd purchased an airplane ticket for me to visit him in New York to celebrate."

She couldn't imagine where this story was going, but she wished he'd hurry up and get to the end of it. Maybe then she'd know what was going on—what had him so upset.

"My mother was furious, but I went anyway. She said my stepfather would try to get me to work in his business, and once I signed on, I'd have sold my soul to the devil himself."

"That's rather harsh, don't you think?" Confusion overshadowed her curiosity. "Is that what you think? I mean, obviously Howard Hughes isn't your stepfather since you're close to his age, so you didn't go to work in the family business, so-to-speak, right?" She laughed softly but sobered quickly when his jaw tightened and his index finger tapped a Morse-code cadence on his knee.

The clock ticked several times before he continued.

"Please let me finish this next part before you ask questions or jump to any conclusions." It was almost a plea. When she shrugged and nodded, he continued, "I doubted my mother. She said he'd try to use me, but I couldn't imagine Vince doing such a thing."

A chill ran down her back even as a silent prayer winged heavenward that the wounded man mentioned in the newspaper wasn't his stepfather. Vince Giovanni. She asked divine intervention that this wasn't what had John upset. But she had to know. "W-was your stepfather one of the men shot in New York last night?"

He hesitated, then nodded.

"Oh, I'm so sorry." She leaned over and placed her free hand on his thigh. "He'll be all right, won't he?" How horrible that his stepfather was part of organized crime and now injured.

The thumping in her chest began to ease, but John slid his hand from hers, leaned forward, and braced his elbows on his thighs, his hands clasped together. Again, ignoring her question, he continued.

"The problem is that my mother was right. He— Vince—didn't exactly ask me to join his business, because, after all, my degree is in engineering and useless to him. But exactly like my mother predicted, he did ask me to do him a *little favor*. I saw no harm at the time, but now, I realize I can't live with the arrangement as it is. I need to come clean and tell you everything."

Me?

She leaned back slowly, one hand gripping the material of her skirt while reaching up the other to rub against her chest above her heart. "What do *I* have to do with this whole thing?"

"If your mother were alive, she could explain it better, but the bottom line is…"

John turned slightly and reached out to reclaim her hand, his skin warm and inviting as she released the cotton material and linked their fingers.

"...she married Vince when she was about twenty."

His words slammed into her with enough force to render her helpless and leave her floundering. He had to be joking—but his eyes were serious.

Her breathing became shallow and fast as her mind raced with possibilities, silently screaming for her to run fast and far. She locked her jaws to stop them from chattering, but tightening every muscle in her body couldn't stop the trembling—or the rest of the message.

"Honey, Vince Giovanni is your father."

"No!" She jerked her hand away as she lurched up from the sofa to put distance between them. "I don't believe you. My father was a *policeman*. Shot and killed on the job. My mother would never lie to me. *Never*."

She turned her back on him, shaking her head in denial of his preposterous statement. Why was he doing this? She cared about him—even loved him—and he was ripping her heart to shreds.

A tear rolled down her cheek and then more. She bowed her head, more tears breaching the dam that now failed to hold back the flood that cascaded down to drip off her jaw onto her favorite dress.

No.

She flinched when strong arms came around from behind to wrap her in warmth. "I can't...can't..."

"Honey, I know it's a shock, but it's the truth. He's kept track of you since you were born, making sure you had everything you needed. But for your safety, he allowed you and your mother to remain here, living under her maiden name."

His words hovered in the charged air surrounding her quivering body, then settled in to be absorbed and digested. When she no longer struggled for freedom, his arms relaxed.

Then another thought struck. *How would he know any of this?*

She stepped away from his touch, turning to glare with enough wattage to light the room, her voice monotone. "Were you sent here to watch me? To *spy* on me? Was that the *favor* you were talking about?"

John took a deep breath, rolled his shoulders then shrugged. "Since I was going to be out here anyway to work for Hughes Aircraft, he hoped I'd be willing to let him know if you needed anything. But I've never reported anything to him about your comings and goings," he added quickly.

Surprising.

All she heard was the thundering of her heart. "But you would have called that man if, for instance, I'd lost my job and was unable to buy food. Right?" Without waiting for an answer, she tightened her hands into fists and lowered her chin, even as she glared at him. "That's why you buy the food I cook for our dinners. You're working for him. You're helping him interfere in my life. Then you tell me some trumped-up story and think I'll believe it's the truth. Well," she spat, shaking her head, "you can forget it."

"No. That's not how it is."

He started forward but halted when she retreated a step, only stopping when her legs bumped into the coffee table and her mother's picture fell to the floor with a crash.

"Oh, no." She glanced around at the broken glass then turned back to John, focusing a lethal glare at him like a gun pointed at a target. "Thanks a lot. That's the *only* picture I have of her, and now the glass is broken."

"Hannah, I'm sorry." He moved forward, but she held up a hand, palm out, effectively stopping him in his tracks.

"Just stay away. You've done enough damage already."

"Please believe me, I never wanted to hurt you. And as for the food, I asked you to cook because I like to eat home-cooked meals. It had nothing—and I mean *nothing*—to do with Vince."

She tried, but failed to stop the new flood of tears. "I don't believe you. You're one of *them*…and you're lying. But what I can't understand is what you hoped to accomplish. I don't have anything." She shook her head, reaching a hand out like a stop sign when he stepped toward her again. "Just leave." Intending her demand to be forceful, she cringed when it whispered out, weak and lifeless.

"Hannah, please…"

Her tear-filled glare stopped whatever he intended to say. She had thought of him as a good, clean-cut young man working hard to get ahead in life. Now, she saw a cunning mobster, maybe even a murderer. How could he be part of something like that and then lie to her about why he was showing her so much attention?

With a heavy heart, she faced the facts. He'd lied—not once, but over and over. She had *trusted* him, had been falling in *love* with him, and he'd betrayed that trust.

Hannah pointed toward the front door. "Leave." *Please, Lord, get him out of here before he sees me totally break down. Please.*

John's eyes pleaded, but she remained defiant. When he finally turned and silently walked from the apartment, his whole body slumped as if carrying the world on his shoulders.

She didn't want to believe a word he said, but…

"If he *is* telling the truth about my father, then I fell in love with a mobster, the same as my mother," she whispered, choking on the last word. And it meant her mother had lied to her.

No, I won't believe it. I won't.

She sank to the floor, leaned over until her face was buried in her cotton skirt, and wept.

Chapter Twelve

Hannah knew there was no use going to bed—sleep would be impossible. After crying herself dry, she stooped beside the table, and with a gentle touch, took the picture from the frame and shook the tiny slivers into the trashcan. A folded piece of paper fell with the shards of glass.

"What's this?" The mumbled question accompanied a tight frown as she unfolded the note.

Hannah, my precious and loved daughter,

If you're reading this, then I guess I'm gone and you're alone in the world to face all the challenges and make the decisions that we used to make together. I know you're able to take on that task—forging the path of your life—but I also know that it's so much easier when you have someone at your side to lean on. I had that for a short while but then chose to walk away from all that was familiar and strike out on a new and uncharted path.

"What is she talking about?" Her hands shook, the world becoming unbalanced at her mother's confusing words. "She didn't choose to face life without Dad. He died." She frowned, but continued to read.

I was twenty when I met your father. He was thirty-four, educated, had a fancy job, and money to spend on me, and I fell head-over-heels in love with him at first sight. I know that sounds silly, but it's true. We had a whirlwind romance and married a few weeks later. Your grandmother wasn't happy about the marriage, but we eloped, so there was nothing she could do about it. I've always hated that she was still angry with me when she passed away.

Now comes the difficult part for me to write, and I know it will be even harder for you to read. Please try to understand, and please don't hate me.

"How could I hate my own mother?" She whispered the question, then mashed her lips together and kept reading.

When I married your father, I didn't know what he did for a living. I thought he was in banking or something similar since he always wore a suit. Rereading that sentence, I realize just how much in love and just how naïve I was back then. It took almost a month for me to finally get suspicious. He left home at odd hours of the day and night and was always being picked up and dropped off by other men in suits who drove new sedans. Who has that kind of money at such a young age?

Then one night, we had a big, nasty fight, and I demanded to know if he was cheating on me. I told him he had to tell me what was going on, or I'd walk out the door. To this day, I wonder if it might have been better to just live in ignorance…but I had to know. That's when he told me he was a lieutenant in a mafia family that dealt in gambling and horse racing.

Like lightning on a stormy night, a chill shot through her body, leaving raised bumps on her arms and her teeth chattering. She sank back onto the floor, leaning against the chair while she clenched her jaws together. The words blurred on the page as tears welled up.

John was right?

No.

She closed her eyes and allowed the tears to trickle down her cheeks, no longer trying to hold back the pain of knowing her mother *had* lied to her—for years. Her blind trust had been betrayed.

The wall clock ticked away the minutes as she huddled, allowing a lifetime of lies to wash over her. A faceless policeman in uniform. Her mother, smiling and happy. The front page picture where two men lay dead. The images flashed in the dark void behind her eyelids, each one leaving her more lost, disillusioned...alone.

When the clock chimed the quarter hour, she slowly opened her eyes and lowered her gaze to the damning piece of paper now resting on her lap. She swallowed, wiped her face, and blinked several times to refocus on her mother's familiar, flowing script.

I didn't believe him at first. I thought he was teasing—then I prayed he was joking, but he confessed to keeping me in the dark about his job. He figured I wouldn't understand.

He was right. I was furious, and we fought like a cat and dog shut up in a small room together. He apologized, and I eventually forgave him. Silly, but I was crazy in love with him.

Then, a few months later, I thought I might be pregnant but didn't say anything at first. I wanted to visit the doctor and know for sure. I wanted to plan something special for when I told him. But your father didn't come home that night, and my fancy surprise dinner was ruined. I tried to wait up but eventually fell asleep. It wasn't until the next morning that I found out his boss had been killed at a restaurant the previous afternoon, and he had narrowly escaped out a back door.

Overnight, everything changed. Your father was now the new don, and everyone was murmuring condolences to him and kissing his ring. I'd never been so frightened in my life. Would he be next? Would I see his picture on the front page of the newspaper lying dead in the street?

Her heart pounded. John *was* telling the truth. The frown deepened, and her grip on the paper tightened.

There I was, pregnant and scared out of my wits. What was I going to do? What if the mob attacked while I was in the car with him? What if my child was killed in the deal? I couldn't sleep, couldn't eat, couldn't focus. It didn't take long to know I had to get away—I had to leave the state and go where I could disappear in the crowd. That was the only way I knew to keep you safe. Two weeks later, I slipped out in the middle of the night and took the train here to Los Angeles.

I named you Hannah Marie Montgomery, using my maiden name. My original plan was to never tell you about your real father, but I've agonized over the years about taking this secret to my grave. It's not that I've had a change of heart—I still don't want you around your father—but guilt is a lonely bed partner. I know you'll wonder why I made the choices I did, but it's difficult, if not impossible, to put my turmoil into words. I can't even fully explain why I've chosen to write this down, but if you ever find my notes, I pray you'll at least try to understand why I had to keep you away from him. You have every right to hate me, but please forgive me for all the lies over the years.

I love you so much,
Mother

Hannah squeezed her hand into a fist, crushing the paper. Was this all a sick joke? Her mother was saying her father was part of the *mafia*. If only she could refuse to believe, or wake up from this nightmare, but with every word, it confirmed what John had told her. She thought back to the newspaper article. If it *were* true, one of those horrible men was her father.

The thought chilled her skin from head to foot. It really didn't matter which one, but John had given her a name. Vince Giovanni.

She lost count of the times the wall clock bonged the half-hour and then the hour. Finally, cold and numb, her energy nearly depleted, she rose from the floor and stood in the middle of the living room. What had once been a safe haven was now almost unrecognizable in the hazy fog of her mind. She stood and turned in a circle, staring at all the familiar things, feeling empty, detached, and lost.

Without consciously focusing on putting one foot in front of the other, she dragged her body into the bedroom and sank down on the edge of the quilted covering. Her hands slid across the knotted squares, then curled into fists to grip the material and hold on while her body trembled.

Did she want to know any more details? No. Could she ignore what she'd read and what John had told her? No. Should she accept it and just move on?

How can I move on without knowing for sure what's real and what isn't?

Her father was really still alive? She shook her head, fighting against reality. Sadly, she admitted the answer. *Yes, he is.* She lifted a hand to press against a suddenly tight chest. Mafia. Her breaths now came quick and shallow, each one a desperate struggle to survive the overwhelming feeling of being crushed under a heavy weight. Pain like she'd never known before radiated across her chest, leaving her tense and gasping for air.

Calm down. Breathe in…one, two, three. Breathe out…one, two, three.

Gradually, she relaxed, reluctantly beginning to accept her mother and John's explanations.

In total defeat, she lowered her chin until it rested on her chest. With eyes closed, she wept out all the pain of years without a father, but the lifetime of lies her mother had told were the arrow that truly pierced her heart.

****

John's world was imploding. He'd heard the clock strike midnight while he lay in bed, exhausted after hours of thinking about Hannah. Even the normally simple task of rolling over had become a chore.

His mind refused to allow the temporary peace of sleep, even though he was mentally exhausted. If only he could go back in time and make different choices—if he could just relive the past couple months. Numb, he lay staring at the ceiling, listening to the alarm clock's faint ticking sound documenting the seconds, minutes, and sadly, hours.

He replayed the evening over and over in his mind, wondering if he could have—*should have*—handled the situation differently.

He couldn't blame Hannah for being upset and not wanting to believe him, but sooner or later, she'd have to realize he'd told her the truth. After analyzing the evening several times in his mind, he realized it hurt that she thought he would ever be involved with the mafia and all the illegal things done by the various different families.

Did she really think he could kill a person?

John gave up trying to sleep and got out of bed. Pacing the cool floor even felt good at this point. While he warmed a cup of leftover coffee, he gave in to the internal struggle to stay as far from Vince and his organization as humanly possible. He was running low on real milk but poured a small amount in the mug and carried it with him to the phone in the hallway. He had to know if Vince was still okay and safe at home under protection. Within minutes, the call was connected.

"Hi. It's me. How's he doing?"

"Hey, boy," Leo greeted. "Yeah, yeah, he's doing okay. He'll be fine. Near miss this time. He's already barking orders and grouchy 'cause Doc says to stay in bed for at least a few days." The bodyguard's chuckle ended on a wheeze that spoke of too many cigarettes.

"I'm glad to hear it. Tell him I called, okay?"

"Yeah, yeah. I'll do that. You be careful, you hear?"

"Thanks."

He hung up the phone, wondering if there was a reason to be concerned. Why had Leo told him to be careful? Did they think someone was after Vince and his family? If so, they'd blown a good chance to take him out when they'd only hit the don in the shoulder.

Was there reason to think they knew about Hannah? He'd need to be a little more alert to their surroundings and anyone who might be hanging around.

With a heavy sigh, he pushed away from the wall and took a step toward her apartment. He stopped at her door, his hand already rising to knock when he remembered the time. Still, concern left him tempted to knock just to check if she was all right, but common sense made him hesitate. Even if she answered, she'd probably slam the door in his face. She'd need time to come to terms with life from this new perspective before she could consider giving him—giving *them*—another chance.

Resigned, John turned toward his apartment. At least he could try helping the healing process by explaining his side—something he hadn't been given a chance to do before being told to leave.

Back in his apartment, he sat down at the small desk in the corner and took out a pen and paper.

Chapter Thirteen

Hannah was up before dawn, sitting at the table with a half-cup of lukewarm coffee and a headache pounding like a base drum in a John Philip Sousa marching band.

She closed her eyes and massaged a throbbing forehead, then ran her fingers up into her matted hair and pulled it taunt for a few seconds before releasing it. The aspirins were finally beginning to help but had a long way to go.

"I've got to get to the market for Mr. Nolan," she murmured, yawning as she rose with coffee cup in hand.

A piece of folded white paper on the floor just inside the door caught her attention. Normally, she got excited at receiving mail, but this morning, she stared at it with foreboding. Her mother had lied to her. Strike one. Her real father was a mafia don. Strike two. Someone had slid a note under her door. Strike three? She didn't feel up to handling another crisis.

With trembling fingers, she stooped to pick up the paper and sent up a silent prayer that there wasn't another catastrophe to deal with.

Tentatively, she eased onto a dinette chair and read.

Hannah,

I'm probably the last person you want anything to

do with at the moment, but I hope you'll read this with an open mind.

As I told you, I was young when my mother married Vince. For the first time in my life, I had a father—or at least a father figure. For the first time, there was someone to teach me to play baseball, to ride a horse, and even a few bad things like how to play poker and keep secrets from my mother about the money he slipped me occasionally. Suffice it to say, I revered the man. He could do no wrong.

Also, as I told you, a few years later, my mother moved the two of us back to Mobile. I didn't know why at the time, and I was hurt that Vince never came to visit me. I didn't hear from him for five or six years— until I graduated high school.

To shorten this story, let's just say I was over the moon to get that call. He said I was an adult now and could make my own decisions. That also sounded good to me, so, of course, I agreed when he offered me college. My dream of designing planes was within my reach.

I heard from him occasionally during those years, but only a note of encouragement and a little cash to help out with any extra expenses.

Then I graduated. I don't know if you can imagine how I wanted to please the only man to pay any attention to me, encourage me, and offer me a chance to fly. There aren't enough words to explain, but all he ever asked in exchange was help to be sure his daughter was okay. I was never to tell you about him, only let him know if things became unsafe or unstable in your life.

That seemed innocent enough at the time.

You see, even though I didn't like the idea—and despite my mother telling me I'd sold my soul to the devil—I wasn't taking money from Vince, so I saw it as a favor, not a job.

I arrived at the boardinghouse and, well, there's an Italian phrase for the first time I saw you. "Un colpo di fulmine." It means, love at first sight, like a bolt of lightning striking. I couldn't get you out of my mind. I wanted more time with you than once a week when you collect the rent. (Speaking of rent, Vince waived my rent, but to me, that was the same as being an employee and receiving pay, so I put a stop to it immediately, and I pay rent to you each week, as you know.) I really don't know how to cook, and sharing a meal was also a good way to spend that extra time with you.

You've been hurt. On the heels of losing your mother, I tell you that she lied to you all your life about your father. That must be hard to hear and even harder to believe. I suggest that you not take anyone's word, but check it out for yourself. There must be official records you can look at.

If I can help in any way, please allow me the opportunity, since I hate having kept the truth from you for as long as I did. I'd like to make it up to you.

Regardless, know I'll always be here for you and be holding out hope that someday you'll forgive me.

John

Hannah's hands shook as she skimmed the letter a second time. John was the first man to give her butterflies in her stomach—the first to make her feel cared about and special. But, like Cinderella in her mother's book of fables, how quickly her carriage had turned back into a pumpkin.

She folded the paper and stood. Now was not the time to ponder the letter or worry about what he thought or felt. Her tenant needed his groceries early.

Within thirty minutes, she was dressed, had brushed her hair, and done what she could to cover the ravages of a night spent crying. After a piece of toast for breakfast, she glanced in the mirror and then started out the door. Her gaze was immediately drawn downward to newspaper-wrapped flowers leaning up against the door frame. A sigh slipped out. Not just any flowers, but three red roses surrounded by delicate, white Baby's Breath.

"Oh my," she whispered, stooping to pick up the flowers as if lifting an infant from a cradle.

She allowed her eyelids to close slowly as she took a slow, deep breath. Her heart drummed, but a quick glance across the hall assured her that no one watched her discovery—and unexpected pleasure. She'd never had a man give her flowers before John—and he gave her roses. Her body tingled, excitement welling up inside like effervescent champagne pushing against a cork.

But, he had spied on her for the mafia—and lied about it.

Her lips pressed into a thin line even as she spun around and reentered her apartment. Regardless, the flowers were beautiful and smelled heavenly. With her bottom lip curled between her teeth, she unwrapped the newspaper and gently added the blooms to the vase with the single rose he'd given her last night.

"I'll arrange them later," she murmured, grabbing her purse before rushing out the door.

On the way to the market, she replayed the events

leading up to telling John to leave her apartment. She stopped watching the few people out walking so early on a weekend and allowed her thoughts to focus inward to debate her current situation.

She'd watched actors and actresses for years and knew how to read their expressions when the director told them to portray a specific emotion. The previous evening, John's face had displayed a wide range of feelings. Hurt and anguish were easy to discern, but he'd hid them quickly. Others were a bit more difficult to detect once he'd raised his guard. But an upset person's voice told the true state of his or her feelings. And his had been concerned and sincere. He'd spoken the truth—even though it put him in a bad position with her.

She was almost to the market when she finally admitted she still trusted him—despite him being sent by Vince Giovanni, her...*father*.

Did she believe that? John had asked her to have an open mind and check it out for herself. He had thrown down a gauntlet.

"There's no choice but to answer his challenge," she mumbled, no longer sure which way she hoped this would end.

If John was right, her father was mafia, but alive. If wrong, then her real father was either dead, as her mother told her over the years, or still out in the world somewhere, and she had no way of knowing how to find him. Did she even *want* to find him?

Yes—and no. There would be no rest for her soul until she found the answers—until she knew for sure. But if investigation proved her father was a mafia don, she didn't want to ever see him.

She decided she'd call and ask her boss for Monday off work. He'd understand if she told him there were a couple family issues to attend to related to the death of her mother.

Well, that's certainly true.

After doing Mr. Nolan's shopping and delivering the groceries to him, Hannah returned to her apartment. The atmosphere had changed. John had filled the emptiness left after the loss of her mother, but the emptiness had returned.

She picked up the letter from the table and reread what he'd written. Only then did it hit home what he'd said about his feelings for her.

" 'There's an Italian word for the first time I saw you,' " she read aloud. " '*Un colpo di fulmine*. It means, love at first sight, like a bolt of lightning striking.' " She sank down to perch on the edge of the sofa, stunned. "How could I have missed his declaration of love?"

Hannah lifted a hand to cover her mouth and shook her head. Could this be happening? Before the previous evening, she would have been excited beyond her wildest dreams, but now... Could she believe this declaration of love—or was he just trying to get back into her good graces so she'd keep allowing him to come over for dinner, and therefore give him the opportunity to keep an eye on her?

Her mind in turmoil, she was unable to sit still, choosing to wander the apartment, touching a memento, picking up a treasured book, but always returning it and moving on.

"This has got to stop."

After making a cup of hot tea, she sat down at the

table and unfolded the previous day's newspaper. The headlines shouted the death of two gangsters in New Jersey, giving details about their respective family businesses and detailing the lives of each man. The reporter suggested that a similar mob hit in New York the previous night was related—a hit where Vince Giovanni had been wounded.

Never interested in the lives or activities of the mafia in the past, she was surprised to find herself fascinated, following the article when it continued on page six. There was a brief mention of Vince previously being married to Sarah Beth Montgomery, though no mention of children.

One more confirmation—one more nail in the coffin.

Do I have relatives?

She'd always wondered about aunts, uncles, or cousins, but her mother and father had been only children—or so she'd been told all her life. Was that also a lie?

Whether it was the truth or not didn't matter. If her father was this Vince person, she wanted nothing to do with his side of the family. As far as she was concerned, he'd been dead all her life, and he'd remain that way.

The phone rang in the hallway outside her door, but she didn't move to answer it. Nothing seemed important anymore. It soon stopped ringing, and she was alone again with her thoughts.

The city continued to live and breathe outside the walls that rose up to keep her protected. Horns honked and people came and went, but inside her safe haven, Hannah huddled in the corner of the sofa and stared at the table where her mother's picture had been displayed for almost five years.

Who had that woman been? Who could fall in love with a mobster?

Then she thought of John. Easy. *She* had, hadn't she?

Like mother, like daughter.

Tears dampened her cheeks. For all she knew, he was right in the middle of this mess—a mafia member sent to watch over her like an avenging angel.

Someone knocking on her apartment door jerked her out of the melancholy pit where she hid. She shifted her gaze in the direction of the disturbance, but remained inert.

"Hannah, answer the door. I know you're in there."

John. She put both hands over her ears.

"Hannah, you're frightening me. Please open the door. We need to talk."

If she had the energy, she might have moved, but standing would require too much effort. She closed her eyes and willed him to go away and leave her alone. She needed time to think, to come to terms with the loss of her mother—at least the mother she'd once trusted and believed in with every fiber of her being. Her mind envisioned ripping a cloth into long strips—shredding it with her bare hands until it lay in a heap at her feet. That heap was her heart, her memories, her life.

****

John gave up trying to get Hannah to open the door. He'd yelled and then, after a deep breath and with determination, he'd cajoled. All without success. He could only imagine what she was thinking or feeling.

Actually, I have no clue.

He turned away, reentered his apartment, and slammed the door. The loud bang helped a bit but didn't solve a thing. The flowers were no longer at her door, so at least he could presume she'd read his letter. More than likely, it hadn't made a difference. She probably didn't believe him—and he didn't blame her.

"Why should she trust me?" The words were mumbled into the silent room.

He stood just inside the door, staring at the sparse furnishings. This wasn't living—only existing. Dinner with Hannah and discussing their daily lives was what life was all about.

Sharing. Loving. Giving.

The apartment appeared smaller than usual and as faded as the aging sofa. His breathing even seemed loud in the silent tomb he called home.

No, not home.

Love lived in homes, and this apartment held none.

John left the empty tomb, tromped down the stairs, and out the front door without a backward glance. With food at the top of the list, he turned right and headed for the diner down the street. A good meal and then—and then maybe he'd go to a bar and forget his troubles.

****

Several hours later, John shuffled home, sick to his stomach and wishing he'd never gone to the pub. The sour taste of the beer on top of his breakfast of eggs and toast had not only been a challenge to swallow, at first, but had then churned his stomach into a frenzy.

The seven-step climb to the front door took every bit of strength and stamina he had left. With his head pounding like jungle drums, he silently prayed to make it to his room before starting to wretch.

Just inside the front door, he stopped when Mr. Nolan stepped out of his apartment with a bag of garbage in his hand. "Lord almighty, son, you look like death warmed over."

He didn't feel like being neighborly. "Yes, sir. It was a rough night." *And morning.* He sidestepped the older man and continued toward the stairs.

"You been seeing our little landlady," he stated. "Hope this doesn't mean you two are fighting or anything."

At least the man was polite while being nosy.

He drew in a slow, deep breath. "Not exactly," he tossed over his shoulder as he started up the steps, hanging onto the railing for all he was worth.

"Good, good, 'cause I'd hate to see her upset. That little ray of sunshine's been through too much already. Yep, too much," he mumbled, forcing his awkward gait to slowly carry him down the hall toward the door leading out to the garbage cans.

John hesitated, glanced down at Hannah's champion, then turned around and made his way back down. "Mr. Nolan, here," he said, taking the bag of garbage from the arthritic-hands. "I'll take this out for you."

"Why, thank you kindly, son."

John unlocked the back door and stepped outside to put the trash in the can. Half-expecting the old gentleman to be waiting to talk, he was thankful to find the lobby empty upon his return. He started up the stairs while considering what to do next. He definitely needed to do something about the girl, but he was in no condition to knock on her door now, not to mention not wanting her to see him in this condition.

He unlocked his door, slammed it behind him, and stumbled into the bedroom before he eased down on the bed, toed off his shoes, and gently lay back on the rumbled sheets.

Tomorrow was soon enough.

Sometime later, John woke in a sweat-drenched panic, breaths coming in short pants as he recalled the dream where he and Hannah ran as hard as they could, but were unable to reach the tunnel where Vince stood calling out for him to take care of his little girl.

A glance at the clock told him it was still early afternoon, but the likelihood of getting back to sleep was slim, if not impossible. Besides, if he slept anymore now, he'd be up half the night.

He kicked at the twisted sheets until his legs were free, then sat on the side of the bed and flexed his toes in the furry rug under his feet.

Hannah.

Was she okay? He wanted to go pound on her door again, but didn't want to draw the attention of all the neighbors, and besides, she probably still wouldn't open to him.

After a visit to the bathroom and a splash of cold water on his face, he wandered into the kitchen to make a cup of coffee. While it brewed, he sat at the tiny dinette table and rested his head in his hands. At work, the current plane being designed and tested was at a critical stage. He needed to spend a little time on the project to be ready for Monday, but that would require being alert and able to concentrate. If that was going to happen, he'd soon have to confront Hannah and...*and what?*

John ran a hand over his mouth, shaking his head.

His deception—withholding the truth for so long—had been a mistake. No—agreeing to keep an eye on Hannah had been his *first* mistake. Withholding the truth after she told him about her fantasy father had been the mistake of all mistakes. No wonder she didn't trust him—didn't want to be around him anymore.

He'd never intended to hurt her, but that was the end result, and the reason she hated him now.

The knock at his door came as a surprise. With the building's front door now locked, it had to be one of the tenants—but, unless there was an emergency, only one person would knock on his door.

He bolted from the chair, bumping it backward to ram into the kitchen cabinet as he made it to the door in three strides. Without hesitation, he swung it open, relief and excitement washing over him like an ocean wave. Her eyes, red and puffy from an obvious night of crying, stopped all forward motion, gripped his stomach, and twisted. If only he could take her in his arms to comfort and protect—if only he could tell her everything would be all right and truly believe those words, but he hesitated.

She stared at him with dark, innocent eyes, like a timid doe ready to flee.

"Hi." He was unsure what else to say.

Hannah glanced at the floor then dragged her gaze back up to meet his. After clearing her throat, she stood a fraction taller and lifted her chin an inch. "I'm sorry," she began. "I've had some time to think about what you said last night…and then I read what you wrote."

He stepped back and lifted an arm to indicate she was welcome to enter. Hesitant at first, she slowly walked in, but stopped a few steps beyond him and just stood in the middle of the room.

"I've made coffee. Come sit down, and we'll talk."

She nodded and preceded him to the table where she slid onto a chair and sat with her hands clenched in her lap.

Adrenalin coursed through his system at seeing her total defeat. He curled his fingers into fists at his side, wanting—needing—to slay the dragon responsible for her pain, yet knowing he was largely at fault.

Fighting the urge to again beg for her forgiveness, he turned to the cupboard, fumbling slightly as he set out two coffee cups and saucers. With an unsteady hand, he filled them and added a dollop of milk to each one before setting them on the table.

"Thanks."

His mind whirled while they both sipped. Should he start the conversation or wait for her? Thankfully, she made the decision for him.

"Thank you for the roses. I've never been given flowers by anyone besides you. They're lovely."

"You're welcome." He didn't need to tell her the store didn't carry flowers, but one of their neighbors down the street had bushes in her yard and agreed to sell him a few for twenty-five cents.

"Um, like I said before, I've given some thought to what you wrote." She took a deep breath and slowly released it before continuing. "Last night, I found a letter from my mother, telling me about my father, although she didn't mention a name. She said he was mafia and that she left him and came to California for my safety. She even asked me to forgive her for the years of lies. I now understand why you kept secrets from me—assuming Vince is really my father. But I must admit, the whole thing, everyone's part in the lies and deception, feels like a huge betrayal. I don't hate you, but it still hurts."

Her words slammed into his chest with the force of a fist. Involuntarily, his hand came up to rub over his heart. "I'm glad you don't hate me, but please know I'm sorry about this whole situation."

She shrugged, turning her cup around in the saucer. "From what you said, if not you, then he'd have had someone else snooping around in my life." Immediately, her gaze rose to connect with his, even as she cringed, pressing her lips together before commenting. "I'm sorry about that comment."

He couldn't stop the chuckle that popped out. "Don't worry about it. Besides, it's true."

"And they might not have had a conscience nagging at them to tell me the truth," she added with a sigh, then focused her gaze on him again. "So, what's next? What should I do?"

He frowned. "What should you do?"

Her brows drew together and her jaw tighten, yet she hesitated, as if searching for words. She focused on her coffee for several heartbeats, but finally lifted her gaze to meet his. "My whole life has been a lie. I don't feel like the same person."

"Oh." He reached out to lay his hand over hers, feeling her fingers tremble beneath his touch. "Hannah, you're definitely the same person, but I think I can understand feeling off balance." He hesitated, but when she remained silent, he continued. "One day at school, years ago when my mother and I lived with Vince, some of the kids started taunting me about being a mobster's kid. They asked how many people I'd shot and other outrageous things. I didn't know what Vince did for a living, so I didn't understand why they had turned on me. I only knew my world had come off its axis."

She nodded. "I'll have to work on forgiving my mother a lifetime of lies, but my father... How do I forgive him? He was never here for me. My friends all had fathers, but I was an outsider."

John sipped his coffee, taking time to think before speaking. He mentally ached for her pain, but his stomach twisted into a knot when her lost-child eyes silently pleaded with him for answers.

He hesitated another moment, seeking a higher power's help. *Give me the right words.* "Well, there's a question I'd like to ask that might help."

"Okay, what?"

"If it were possible, would you want to go back to the time when you thought your father was a dead policeman and your mother a sainted woman who always told the truth? Would you want to go back to living in the fantasy world your mother created?"

She sat taller with her shoulders back and eyes growing dark and stormy. "Yes. I was happy then."

He glanced at her hands gripping the cup tight enough to turn her knuckles white. "I know your world is upside down right now, but think about this. When I first moved here, you told me about two parents who had loved you, but were both deceased. Your mother moved here, lying to give you a sense of security and maintain your safety. Your father isn't a deceased policeman, a hero, but a man working outside the law, and for your safety, he allowed you to remain here. Hannah, both of your parents made certain decisions…because of their love for *you*."

"What do you mean?" Her eyes narrowed, but thankfully, she was listening.

"Your mother left the man she loved and moved to another state in order to keep you safe. The man she left, Vince, let her remain hidden away here on the west coast because he loved her and you. He put distance between himself and you—gave up the woman he loved and a future child—just to keep the two of you *safe*."

Her pursed lips began to relax and soften around the edges. When her pupils began to constrict and her shoulders sag, he silently thanked his lucky stars he was reaching her.

"Hannah," he cajoled, reaching out to touch her hand again, "he could have come out here and dragged her back to New York. Or your mother could have been selfish and remained with Vince, and then you would have been raised in New York, living in a compound—a fortified home—surrounded by tall, thick walls. And, I might add, a dozen other men living in or near the compound, and all of them wearing guns strapped under their jackets in order to protect you and your parents—with their very lives, if necessary."

She leaned away from him, her eyes dark and huge, blinking several times as the blood drained from her face.

"Can you imagine what your life would have been like?" he pressed on. "Your mother would have worried herself sick every time Vince went out without her. Was he going to kill someone, or maybe be killed himself? Or maybe he'd be arrested and thrown in prison. But what if they went out together? She'd have worried herself sick for fear someone would attack him, and maybe that she'd be killed also, leaving you an orphan. Can you imagine the life of a don's wife and child?"

"No," she whispered, her hand coming up to cover her mouth.

Like the sun flooding a room when a curtain is opened, for the first time, John himself fully realized what his own mother had given up for *his* safety. She had sacrificed her happiness and left the man she loved—possibly still loved on some level—to protect her son. The thought left him humbled.

He blinked several times, drawn back from the past to face the present. "Hannah, good or bad, your parents are who they are, and each made decisions that impacted your life—not selfishly, but because they *loved* you. My own mother loved Vince but took me away from him and New York, too, because she feared what he did for a living and feared I'd follow in his footsteps."

"But he cared about you. He helped *you* and paid for *your* college."

"Yes, and I'm grateful, but he helped you also."

"No," she countered, frowning while she shook her head in denial.

"Yes." In earnest, he gently tightened his fingers around hers. "He had someone watching you and your mother to be sure you were safe and didn't need anything. I also wouldn't be surprised if he had something to do with your mother getting the manager's job here."

"No, you're wrong. She applied for the job. Vince had nothing to do with it."

His frustration level inched up a notch. *Vince*

176

should be the one explaining, not me.

She closed her eyes again, as if putting a shield between herself and the pain. "This is unbelievable."

When next she opened them, it saddened him to watch the blue gaze radiate the same emotions he'd often seen in his mother's eyes: loss and anguish— something he didn't know how to alleviate.

"It's like being an actor in a movie, but without a script. How can I go in front of the camera without knowing what's coming next in the story?"

Tears trickle down her cheeks, ripping at him, yet leaving him hesitant to offer comfort. With a slowly drawn breath, he made the decision.

John stood and stepped around the small table. As if in slow motion, he reached out and took her hand, tugging gently until she stood. Relief was palatable when she not only allowed his arms to encircle her, but stepped in to lean against him, turning her head just enough to rest her cheek against his chest.

This is where he wanted her—now and forever.

Forever.

Where had his sub-conscience gotten that thought? Forever meant marriage and kids. Maybe too soon to be thinking along those lines considering...

"Where do I go from here?"

The whispered question left him pondering, not sure what to suggest. She wanted him to lead, but he was stepping out into uncharted territory, and from his point of view, the ground looked swampy and filled with pitfalls. He'd need to proceed with caution.

"You've had quite a shock and probably need some time to process all of this." He felt her nod. "My suggestion is that you go down to the courthouse, or county records, and look up your birth certificate. Maybe ask for a marriage license. That might answer all your questions, and then we can talk more after that."

She leaned away from him and stared up into his eyes. "That makes a lot of sense. Get the facts and then decide what I want to do next—if anything. Maybe letting life roll on as before is the best thing to do."

"It would certainly be the easiest, but I'm not sure that would satisfy you. But for now, just get the facts, and then you can make a decision based on those and, hopefully, not just on emotions. Okay?"

She hesitated, then nodded.

"Good."

"Thanks for the coffee." She stepped away, offering a shy, tired smile. "See you for dinner tonight?"

A weight fell from his shoulders. "Yes, I'd love that." He walked with her to the door and watched until she unlocked her apartment and stepped inside, glancing back to wiggle her fingers in a tiny wave before closing it.

John glanced toward the ceiling, thankful and seeking a little divine help in her struggles.

The hours would creep by until he could see her again.

Chapter Fourteen

After a quiet dinner with John, and a second sleepless night, Hannah was more than ready to get proof. She had arranged for the day off and now stood in the warm, early-morning sun outside the Hall of Records building, peeking through the glass and waiting for someone to come open the door for business. Normally patient, she felt antsy and nervous. Would she find proof her father was Charles Thomas Montgomery, former policeman, or Vince Giovanni, the mafia don?

A plump woman scurried across the building's lobby, twisted a key in the lock, and pushed open the door. "Good morning, and how can I assist you today?"

"I'm here to look at my birth certificate."

"You were born in California?"

"Yes, ma'am."

The lady beamed. "Good, then we can help you. Just go up these stairs, dear," she said, pointing, "and talk with the woman at the counter."

"Thank you."

Hannah reached the top of the steps, a little anxious, but determined.

"May I help you?"

"I'm looking for my birth certificate."

The young woman behind the counter smiled and handed her a form. "Please fill this out and return it to me. If you plan to wait, I'll research it immediately. Thankfully, we have the past twenty-five years here in the file room, so since you're first in line, it shouldn't take more than half an hour."

Thirty-five minutes later, she stared down at her birth certificate.

Born: Hannah Marie Montgomery.

Mother: Sarah Elizabeth Montgomery.

Father: Unknown.

Hannah frowned, sucked in a deep breath, and imagined herself lashing out at a cruel world. Just as quickly, her shoulders slumped and tears welled up. She just wanted her life to return to normal.

Clearing her throat, she cast a quick glance at the clerk before taking one last look at the document. "Thank you," she whispered, turning her back and stepping away before whirling back around. "Can I check for a copy of a marriage license?"

"Certainly. Just fill out this other form, please."

The second request took twice as long. An hour later, she followed the worn path in the linoleum until she stepped out into the sunshine.

She had nothing. No birth certificate with a father's name and no marriage certificate for Sarah Elizabeth and Charles Thomas Montgomery. Her world had closed in to weigh her down and leave her wondering where to turn next.

At the corner, she went inside the Woolworth Company and sat down on a stool at the counter.

"What can I get for you, miss?"

She glanced up at the middle-aged woman with neat curls and clean, white apron. "Just coffee with milk."

"Coming right up. We only have reconstituted powdered milk. I hope that's okay?"

She nodded, not really caring one way or the other. Once served, she stirred a dollop of milk into the hot, black liquid, her mind barely noting the rich aroma. Her mother had lied about everything.

No, wait a minute.

Her back straightened and her hands stilled. Maybe there *had* been a Charles Montgomery who worked for the Los Angeles Police Department?

She left the coffee untasted, slid a nickel under the edge of the saucer, and headed toward the back of the store where a sign on the wall advertised the location of a phone booth.

Once inside with the door closed, she dialed the operator. "Los Angeles Police Department, please."

The connection was almost immediate.

"Hello. How can I assist you?"

"I need to find out if a Charles Thomas Montgomery ever worked as a policeman for Los Angeles. He would have been killed in action about twenty-three years ago."

"It'll take a while to look that up in our logs. Can you call back in an hour or two? Just ask for Sybil."

"Yes, thank you."

****

The trolley ride was long. After a stop at the corner market to get a newspaper and a few items, including powdered milk for one of her tenants, Hannah walked the short distance home, surprised when she suddenly stood at the bottom of the porch stairs, looking up the steep mountain she needed to climb. With an arm around the bag and a hand on the railing, she forced one foot in front of the other until she'd reached the first floor. After delivering the milk, she dragged her weary body up the next flight of stairs and closed herself in her lonely apartment.

She put the food in the refrigerator, then slipped out to the phone and dialed the police department. After three rings, a young woman answered.

"I'm Hannah Montgomery. Is this Sybil?"

"Oh yes, but I'm sorry to tell you that we don't show a Charles Montgomery ever working for the department. Is there anything else I can help you with?"

"No. Thank you." She hung up the phone and wandered back into her apartment.

Defeat had stolen her last ounce of enthusiasm. She'd never felt more depressed and alone. More and more it appeared that everything her mother had written and John said was the truth. Her father wasn't a hero; he was a hoodlum and murderer—a man who lived on the opposite side of the law.

In her mother's bedroom, she stopped in front of the mirror to stare at her reflection. "Do I resemble him in any way?"

Not in morals, that's for sure.

Hannah frowned at herself and turned away, drifting into the living room and turning on the radio before settling on the sofa. The whole subject of her parents still weighed heavy on her mind, but she forced her thoughts away from the painful subject and focused on John instead.

The night before had started out much like the very first night they ate spaghetti together—quiet and uncomfortable—but once they began discussing his work, the tension eased and the evening was enjoyable.

Then he'd stood to leave.

The memory sent warmth spreading across her chest, up her neck, and onto her face. He had taken her in his arms, holding her with gentle firmness until she relaxed against his warmth and strength.

With a smile, she burrowed back against the cushions and closed her eyes. The more she thought about John, the more she knew there was no way he could be involved in killing anyone. Her life had been turned upside down, but if anyone could help her get back the balance, it was him. He may have lied by omission in the beginning, but everything he had confessed since had turned out to be the truth.

She might be making a huge mistake, but her mind was made up—she trusted him and was willing to follow his lead.

Chapter Fifteen

Hannah slept in fits and starts, pulling the covers up to her chin while she shivered, then kicked them off when she woke sweating. In an endless battle to conquer her demons, she remained in bed long after she knew there would be no more sleep for her that night. She hated admitting defeat.

With burning eyes and a heavy heart, she slipped on a Chenille robe and headed for the kitchen. She ran water into the coffee pot, then scooped grounds into the basket before setting it on the stove to percolate. The bag of coffee Mr. Hughes had given John was almost gone, but they had really enjoyed the reprieve from Postum. Although better than nothing, it really was a low quality substitute for real coffee.

While it brewed, she sat down at the small table and leaned her head forward to rest on her hands. With eyes closed, she rubbed her forehead and fought tears that threatened to take her current fuzzy, full-headed feeling and help it blossom into a full-fledged, splitting headache.

After John had called the previous night to say he'd be missing dinner because he had to work late, she'd gone to bed early and dreamed about him.

"Well, not a dream…more like a nightmare," she muttered, shivering at the memory of a shadowy figure telling them they were in the mafia and there was nothing they could do about it. At one point, the faceless voice had called her his daughter and said the mafia was in her blood and it did no good to argue the fact.

Thank goodness it had only been a dream, but even now, her thoughts kept returning to John and his denial that he was part of anything to do with the mafia.

He can't be part of the mob. He just can't.

He was gentle and caring. But was he also a good actor?

When the coffee's strong aroma filled the apartment, she stood to pour a cup, then cradled it between both hands and held it under her nose before taking several deep breaths.

The sun was just peeking over the horizon. Fortunately, her boss was understanding when she'd called the afternoon before and arranged a second day off. Now, she could relax with her coffee. The apartment needed to be dusted, and she needed to do laundry, but not today. During the sleepless night, she'd come to a decision, and now wasn't the time to start procrastinating.

With cup in hand, she headed for the bathroom to wash her face and put on enough makeup to hide at least the worst of the restless hours before slipping on a pair of slacks and an over-sized white shirt.

She ran a brush through her hair, smiling at herself in the mirror to see the final effect, then groaned aloud. "This is as good as it's going to get."

After refilling her cup and pouring one for John, she slipped out of her apartment and crossed the hall to knock on his door. She almost took a step back when the door immediately swung inward, and he stood there, larger than life and twice as angry.

"Oh, sorry. I…come in." He smiled when she held out the second cup of coffee. "Please tell me this is for me and you're not just teasing me with that wonderful smell." He accepted the cup after she nodded. "Care to sit on the sofa or at the table?"

"It doesn't matter." But she headed for the sofa and perched on its edge, holding her cup in one hand and running a finger around the rim with the other. "I um…how are you this morning?"

He released a breath and chuckled softly. "I didn't sleep well, if you must know. I was concerned about you." He settled down on the opposite end, turning slightly to face her. "You don't appear to have slept well either. Are you feeling okay?"

She shrugged, taking a sip of coffee before continuing. "I went down to the county building yesterday, looking for a copy of my birth certificate to see who was listed as my father." She relaxed the grip on the cup when he focused intently on her, concern etched in his slight frown.

"Did you find it?"

"No. My mother put 'unknown' on the line instead of my father's name."

He only nodded.

"So, then," she continued, sucking in a breath and holding it a moment before delivering the next bit of evidence that condemned her mother. "I checked for a marriage license for my mother and the man she said had been my father. There wasn't one. Last, I called the police department and asked them to check their records, but the lady couldn't find a Charles Montgomery," she finished with a sigh.

John reached for her cup and, along with his, set them on the coffee table before reaching for her hand and tugging until she scooted closer. Wrapped in his arms, she leaned against his body, allowing his strength to hold her steady and help block out the prior day's disappointments. He radiated heat that seeped in and warmed her chilled skin. With her eyes closed against the world's ugliness and hurt, she slid her arms up around his neck and nuzzled her nose against the softness of his neck. He smelled of shave cream.

She leaned away slightly and studied his clean jawline. "You already shaved this morning. You don't have to leave early for work, do you?"

"No, but I planned to stop by your apartment and check on you, then I was going to walk down to the corner diner and have breakfast. I didn't have the inclination or energy to make my own. Do you have enough time to go with me? I'd love for you to join me so we can talk, but I wouldn't want you to get in trouble."

She couldn't make herself turn down his offer, despite the recent hurt he'd caused. Her smile was weak, but she nodded. "I called work yesterday and arranged a second day off."

He instantly flashed that special smile that melted her heart and sent her emotions into overload.

John held the door for her, and soon they were walking outside in the warm morning. Summer was waning, and the children would be heading back to school within a week, but in the meantime, and despite the early hour, a couple boys played stick ball in the street, running for the sidewalk when a car rumbled by.

Hannah enjoyed watching children play, although

she'd seldom been involved with outside games as a child. Her mother had kept her pretty close to home and constantly under her supervision. With what she'd learned recently, it was easy to imagine how she must have feared her real father finding her and whisking her away.

Her mother had worried for nothing.

"What are you thinking right now?"

Hannah glanced at John, then focused on the sidewalk, trying to avoid the cracks that could trip up a person who wasn't paying attention. "I'm thinking about all the lies and deception, but I'm also thinking about what you asked me the other night. Would I want things the way they were before, and not know the truth?" She blew out a breath. "Truth, at least truth as I knew it, seems to have boarded a plane and taken a one-way flight to parts unknown. I don't seem to know what the truth is any more."

They walked the rest of the block in silence while she pondered her conclusion one last time before continuing. Why was she having such a difficult time sharing her feelings? John had lived through a different, yet similarly unstable situation. She was sure he'd understand, even if he didn't agree with her conclusions or her chosen course of action.

She sighed, knowing why the situation was so hard. If she stated her feelings—and shared her preference of living on as if she'd never been told, then John would think she was hiding and not strong enough to face reality.

And maybe he'd be right.

At the diner, she released her held breath, despite knowing the reprieve would last only a few minutes.

The silence continued while they were seated and their coffee was delivered.

Once their meal was ordered, he leaned forward in the booth, his arms resting on the table while he sipped coffee. "Well?"

The heavy, white mug became her focal point while she gathered her thoughts. When she was ready, she glanced up, relieved to connect with a non-judgmental stare, but she still felt trapped. He wouldn't let her get away without telling him what he wanted to hear.

Easy for him.

An inner groan pushed her forward, despite mentally kicking and screaming like one of the big-screen actresses being dragged away into the dark of night to be held for ransom.

"I've missed having a father all these years, but I've done okay. And this Vince might have had someone watching, but apparently there was no reason for the person to intervene." She waited a couple heartbeats for him to dispute her assumption. When he remained silent, she continued. "So, I'm just going to continue on as before and forget there's any chance he is my real father."

There, she'd said it out loud—and the world was still turning, and she was still breathing, although her breaths were short and shallow, her chest rising and falling faster than she cared to admit. She lifted the mug for a fortifying swallow.

John took a moment before responding. "Hannah, I can't make the decision for you, but I think you should go see your father—go see Vince."

"No!" Immediately, she lifted her gaze to glance

around the cafe, noting a few heads turn to glance in their direction.

"Aren't you even a little bit curious?"

She vigorously shook her head, turning her attention back to the mug of cooling coffee.

"Don't you wonder why he never contacted you or your mother when he obviously knew where you were?"

After another quick glance around the cafe, she leaned forward and spoke just above a whisper. "I don't owe him *anything*. My mother worked hard to raise me and keep a roof over my head. He did nothing. Nothing," she hissed emphatically, glaring at him.

How dare he even suggest she owed that man even a moment of her time? He might be her natural father, but he'd failed when it came to supporting her and being there when she needed anything. Her mother deserved all the credit. Vince Giovanni deserved absolutely nothing.

Her hands were still curled into fists when he spoke again.

"There's a lot I don't know about your father, but I do know a few things."

"Name one," she ordered, her words shoved out between clenched teeth.

"He bought that boardinghouse."

Her mouth dropped open. She couldn't believe it. This couldn't be true.

"That's why I think he might have had a hand in your mother getting the manager's job. The job comes with a rent-free apartment, doesn't it?"

She nodded, but words were impossible as anger flowed from her body like water down a drain. Hannah sagged onto the bench seat, her emotions—the hatred and haughty attitude—dying a rapid and emotionally painful death. "You might be right. He was probably around all along." She closed her eyes and shook her head. "Of course, Mother might have known and chose not to tell me. She didn't mention anything, either way, in her letter, so I have no way of knowing."

"Did you get any help with your schooling to learn to do make-up and hair?"

She lifted her gaze to meet his, her answer hesitant. "I saved some money, and I also had a scholarship."

"After I graduated college and went to New York to visit him, he told me he'd paid for your schooling. Only after talking with you recently did I realize that he must have only paid for a portion, not all of your expenses like he did for me. He owes it to you and needs to make it right."

Her body began to tremble. "No, he owes me *nothing*." She could read the pity in John's eyes. This was obviously painful for him as well, but why did he have to drive another nail into the coffin? The more he told her, the more she realized how much her mother had kept from her. Every good memory was being tainted.

She swiped at a tear cascading down her cheek. Who was she fooling? The damage had been done—she could never go back to an easier and more innocent time. The realization stabbed deep, ripping at her heart.

John nodded as if reading the reluctant acceptance on her face.

"Here you go. One bacon and eggs over easy with toast and one with eggs scrambled." The waitress set the plates in front of them, halting all discussion as they each thanked her, then only stared at the food.

Hannah raised a hand up to rub across her stomach, no longer hungry, but knowing she'd eat, having been trained not to waste food.

They ate in silence for several minutes, but already she could feel the greasy food churning in her stomach. A silent prayer winged heavenward that she'd keep it all down and not embarrass John or herself.

She breathed a sigh of relief when the meal was over and they left the stuffy, odor-filled diner. Outside, she turned her face toward the sun and allowed the warmth to help settle her squeamish stomach. Still, she knew the conversation still hung out over an abyss, unfinished.

What should I do?

She followed his lead when he started walking toward the boardinghouse. John thought she should meet the man and judge for herself—not run and hide. From the distant past, she remembered a time she'd told her mother about being afraid to stand in front of the class and give a book report. She'd never forget her mother's response. *"When you're afraid, that means you either need to be careful of some danger, or it means you need to step up and face that fear and do the very thing you're afraid of. That's the only way to get rid of fear."*

"You're obviously having a tough time with this," John began, breaking the silence. "But I have one last thought, and then I won't bring it up again. Okay?"

She nodded, hoping his comment would help her decide the best thing to do.

"I'm just wondering how you'll feel down the road if you choose not to meet him, and then he's killed some day. Will you regret your decision? When it's too late, will you wish you'd chosen differently and had at least met him?"

She'd never given any thought to seeing the man, and definitely not what she'd think or feel years from now. Would she care if he died, taking away her choice? Suddenly, a shiver ran through her body. Why was John really in Los Angeles, and what all had he agreed to do for that man?

"Did he send you here to get me to *go back* to New York?"

"No," he retorted.

His emphatic denial of her veiled accusation gave her a little reprieve.

"In fact, he swore me to secrecy. I'm breaking a promise by telling you what I know. If, or *when*, he finds out that you know, that's something I'll have to face with him. But I couldn't live any longer keeping things from the woman I'm in love with."

She halted near where he'd need to catch the trolley and turned to stare up into his gaze. "You've implied that a couple of times now, but I'm not sure what those words mean to you." Her heart pounded, praying they meant the same to him as they did to her.

With each passing second, her hopes faltered, and her silent prayer became more fervent.

Finally, John reached out and took her hand. "Love to me, as a youngster, meant someone spending time with me and giving me things. As I grew up, I realized love means that I'd do anything for that person. I'd give my life, if necessary. It also means that I want that person to be with me all the time—every day."

"Would you say you love Vince?"

His brow furrowed, as if in thought, but it didn't take him long to answer. "I care about Vince, but he lives outside my definition of sacrificial love. People who love you unconditionally don't give to get. In other words, they don't pay for your college and then ask you to be a party to lies and deceit." He glanced at his watch before his next comment. "We have time enough for me to walk you to the boardinghouse. Come on."

He reached to take her hand as they walked. The building came into view, standing solid with the morning sun reflecting off the front windows, but today, she actually saw it—actually thought about the building being home. Despite who owned it, it contained happy memories.

Maybe that's what John alluded to—memories made with a person who was willing to sacrifice everything for her was the person deserving her love. Her mother had lied, but she'd loved with all her heart and given up things to keep her safe. Though Hannah wasn't a mother, she could understand that kind of sacrificial love.

John unlocked the boardinghouse door and allowed her to enter first.

Once it was closed behind them, blocking the outside noise of playing children and passing vehicles, she turned toward him. "You've said you love me, but will your feelings change if I choose not to go see Vince as you think I should?"

He stepped in closer, sliding a hand along her waist to reach around and hold her close while he rested his other palm on her cheek. "I don't give love expecting to get you to decide the way I want. I *offer* love," he whispered, "because you're beautiful, inside and out, and I can't imagine life without you in it."

Her heart pounded as he lowered his head, brushed his lips across her cheek, and then feathered kisses down to trail along the jaw to her lips. When his tongue darted out to trace her bottom lip, her legs buckled. His arm tightened to hold her against him while he leaned in to devour her lips.

Her head swam, foggy and confused while groping to focus on the sensations that slammed into her body—sensations she wanted more than her next breath. Sensations she wanted to continue forever. Her arms tingled, and her body floated on a sea of desire and longing.

"Well, bless my soul."

Hannah jerked back at the interruption followed by wheezing laughter that came from behind them.

With as much stealth as possible, she slid her hand from John's grasp. "Oh, hi, Mr. Nolan. We, um, we just got back…" She couldn't remember the last time she'd been this embarrassed.

A quick glance at John showed him recovering from the initial surprise, but then a smile widened as he watched the older man limp forward.

"Child, you don't have to explain anything to me. I'm just glad to see you have a handsome beau who respects you and makes you happy. You two kids go ahead, don't let me stop you," he added, chuckling as he hobbled past and out onto the porch stoop to drop onto a chair.

She watched as the door slowly closed behind him, then looked back at John. His wide grin was contagious, and she started to laugh. He joined in, wrapping an arm around her shoulders and squeezing before stepping away.

"I didn't know we had an audience. Sorry." He looked sincere, although he still had a broad smile.

"It's okay. He's a sweetheart—only grandfather I ever had."

"I'm glad you had someone to fill a void. I had a grandfather, but he wasn't as much fun as Mr. Nolan. Anyway," he said, glancing at his watch, "I've only got a few more minutes with you, and then I'll have to head to the trolley."

"Okay, but I'll miss you." She went up on her toes and brushed a light kiss on his lips. "Before you go, I wanted to tell you that I've thought about your question, and you're right. I should meet the man and form my own opinion. I should give him a chance to tell me his side of things. Besides, it might answer some of the questions I figured would never be answered."

A grin slowly spread across his face. "I'm glad to hear you're willing to face the unknown." He gave her a squeeze. "And I will be there with you, every step. I just hope you get all your questions answered."

She ran her tongue along suddenly dry lips. Was she making a bad decision? What if her father didn't like her, or what if he got angry with John for telling her the truth after he'd promised to keep the man's secret?

With a deep breath, she mentally forced her worries to take a step back. This was a case where John knew more than she did, and she needed to trust him.

"Well, from what you've said, he doesn't know that you've told me about him, so what's the next step? What do we do now?"

Chapter Sixteen

In the back seat of the taxi on the way to the airport, John sat next to Hannah, silently sharing encouragement and strength with an occasional smile and a squeeze when her cold hands started to fidget. She had never looked more stylish than today in her navy-blue, mid-calf suit with white piping that flattered her slender figure and brought out the blue in her eyes. The large-brimmed hat hid most of her thick, dark hair, but small wisps curled around her ears adorned with small pearl earrings.

The lady was a class act, and he wanted her in his life. He'd never felt this way before, and, hopefully, she felt the same.

"How do they know those big things will stay up in the sky?"

He chuckled, sobering when she quirked her mouth to one side and frowned. "Sorry, I wasn't laughing at you. It's just that everyone asks the same question about planes. Look," he said, meshing his fingers with hers, "I could give you a history in the science of aeronautics, but let's just say that the concept is similar to how birds fly, and birds rarely fall out of the sky. Contrary to what people think, it's safer to fly than it is..." He stopped mid-sentence, stomach tightening. How insensitive could a guy be? He'd been about to say flying was probably safer than walking down the street, but that comment would have dredged up her mother's recent death. "Well, safer than any other mode of transportation that I know of."

She remained silent, staring at him for several moments before speaking. "I guess if it were highly dangerous, you wouldn't fly, right?"

"Exactly. Now, don't worry about that and just enjoy a new experience. After all, isn't that what life is all about?"

"I thought it was about a man and woman working together for a better future and raising kids that will be upstanding citizens and a contribution to society."

He turned slightly in the seat to get a better view of her. "That's very philosophical." He chuckled when she smiled and shrugged. "Honey, I know you're nervous about meeting your father, and I don't blame you, but just remember that he loves you."

She stared at him, gaze screaming skepticism, but she remained silent and just nodded.

The air terminal was bustling, but it didn't take them long to hand their two small cases over to the porter and line up to board. He held on to her hand, her nails digging into the back of his being the only outward sign of her trepidation at this new experience—and no doubt, the meeting with her father when they reached New York.

"This terminal is busier than I expected."

"Flying is expensive, but saves a lot of time. Probably most of these men are flying for business reasons. Did you have anything to eat this morning?" She shook her head, but he doubted she was even conscious of lifting her free hand to press against her stomach. "Well, if you're hungry later, they serve water and sandwiches on the plane." Another thought crossed his mind. "Oh, and here's a stick of Wrigley's. Chew half of it when we get ready to take off to help keep pressure from building up in your eardrums. Then as we land, you should chew the other half."

"Okay." The gum disappeared into her purse. "Do you collect the baseball cards that comes with some of the gum?"

He nodded. "I never did before, but this year, the Goudey Gum Company started a History of Aviation series, so I'm hoping to get them all. There's supposed to be ten in the series. Who knows, they might be worth a lot of money someday. With Hughes breaking all kinds of flying records and another long-distance flight planned for next year, his card will be very popular."

Arriving at the counter, he pulled the coupon book from his pocket and handed it to the agent.

"Two flying to New York City." The young man glanced up and smiled. "We have a great DC-3 all lined up. I'm sorry that this flight doesn't have sleeping berths, but the seats are padded and very comfortable. Is this your first flight?"

He watched Hannah nod and even manage a tight smile despite her breathing already coming a little more rapid than normal. But she was facing her fears, and he couldn't be more proud of her.

"Great. You'll enjoy the experience, and I hope you fly with us again soon."

"Thank you, sir." He turned his attention on Hannah. "We don't have long to wait. Do you want anything?"

She shook her head. "No, thanks. So, we won't arrive until about noon tomorrow?"

He led her toward two seats along the wall where they could watch the other passengers until their flight was called. "That's right. It'll take about twenty hours or so, but we land a few times for fuel, and we'll be able to stand up and stretch. I was hoping to get a flight with sleeping berths, but there wasn't one like that available. Sorry."

"That's okay. I know this flight must be horribly expensive, and I imagine having a bed and all would cost even more."

He didn't want to think about how much this flight was costing for two tickets. He'd be scrimping and saving for a year to replace his meager savings that had just been depleted. But she was worth every dime.

The conversation lagged as they watched passengers arrive and depart. He held her hand, squeezing it every so often and smiling when she glanced his way.

"You know," she said, gently waving her free hand to indicate the terminal, "I find it interesting that people can come to an airport and then fly to all different parts of the country. It's like a wheel hub, and planes fly out in all directions like the spokes in that wheel."

"That's exactly what it's like. In fact—"

"The flight for New York is ready to board," the agent behind the counter called out. "Would all passengers with passage on that flight please proceed to the door on my right and walk to the plane parked straight ahead."

"That's us." Hannah sucked in a deep breath.

He nodded. "Are you nervous?"

She hesitated. "A little bit, but since you're with me, I know everything will be okay—not just during the flight," she added, glancing to him with a slight smile, "but tomorrow after we get there."

He stood a little taller. How had he gotten so lucky? Even after admitting his sins to this woman, she still trusted him to have her best interest at heart. What had he done to deserve such loyalty?

Stepping in behind her, he ushered her into the line heading out the door to walk across the asphalt toward the plane.

A smiling young woman in a tailored uniform greeted them. "Good afternoon," she said, shaking their hands. "Welcome to the flight. I hope you enjoy being our guests."

"Thank you."

John followed Hannah as they climbed the steps that had been rolled up to the plane and found their seats.

"You know, I'm beginning to get a little excited." Her smile became less tentative as she took in every detail of the interior. "And we even have a little round window so we can watch the birds."

He grinned and nodded, but refrained from telling her the plane would be flying at about twenty thousand feet above the ground, far above the birds and up among the clouds. No need to worry her sooner than necessary.

John noticed that other than the air stewardess, Hannah was the only woman on board. She kept busy watching the men on the ground adding fuel and putting the small amount of luggage aboard. She no longer looked nervous—until the pilot started up the two big engines. That's when her body tensed and her eyes widened.

"Hold my hand. It'll help hold the plane together if things get shaky."

Her gaze immediately shifted to glare at him, just before she punched him on the arm. "Brat," she whispered.

He didn't bother to stop the chuckle that slipped out as he reached for her hand and gave it a quick squeeze. "Guilty as charged. But just so you're forewarned, it will be a bit shaky and probably even bumpy at times. It's normal, so try not to let it scare you. I'll be right here beside you all the way."

She nodded, and he reminded her to chew half her gum as he put his piece in his mouth.

Her eyes closed when the plane began to roll forward. John tried not to stare, but the urge to see how she was handling this new experience was overwhelming. Her lips pressed together into a straight line, and her chest rose and fell with each shallow breath. The roar from the propellers as they revved for takeoff echoed off the walls of the cabin, creating a constant, loud hum that might seem noisy to her, but, according to what he'd been told, was a great improvements over flying only a few years earlier.

John relaxed his head back against the top of the seat, bracing for the gradual increase in speed and then the surge that would lift them into the air. The plane was now scooting down the runway at a good clip, but he would have been able to tell just by the increase of Hannah's grip on his hand, and how her rounded fingernails dug into his skin.

"Can you count to ten?"

"Hm?" She opened her eyes and turned to stare at him.

"Can you count to ten?" he repeated.

She gave him a disgusted frown. "Of course, why?"

"I just wondered. Oh, and by the way, we're off the ground."

Her head jerked around, and she stared out the small portal. "Hey, we are. Oh, and we're getting higher. And look at all the houses. They're getting smaller. This is fascinating."

The pressure on his hand decreased as she focused on the world outside the plane.

So far, so good.

At least until they had to land. That would probably be another tense time—unless she was sleeping, of course.

He had to smile at her child-like captivation while she sat straighter in the seat to look down at the city as it grew smaller and smaller below them. Thankfully, she was enjoying the thrill of flight and putting concerns about meeting her father on hold. He, on the other hand, had betrayed Vince and broken a promise.

John didn't fear dire consequences, but being disowned and no longer welcome was a definite possibility.

Hannah might be gaining a father, but he stood a good chance of losing one.

Chapter Seventeen

John's gaze focused on the crunch of cars and bicycles clogging the road and slowing their progress in getting from the airport to the hotel, but his thoughts focused on the upcoming meeting. Had it only been a week since he called to warn Vince about their visit? It hadn't taken long to leave the message...

"I'm flying in for a quick visit next Saturday afternoon...and I'm bringing a skirt."

Leo had chuckled. *"Ah, Johnny-boy. You work fast. Coming home to get the old man's approval?"*

"No. I already know he won't approve. Just tell him. Thanks."

He'd hung up on the lieutenant before the other man could say anything else. There was nothing else to say.

He swallowed, glancing over to Hannah.

Not surprising, Vince hadn't bothered to call him back. He'd gotten the message, and John already knew the man's opinion.

He pulled the hankie from his back pocket and wiped his sweaty brow.

"How much longer before we arrive at the hotel?"

"It won't be long now. You were rather quiet on the flight. Are you all right?" He fanned them with a folded newspaper.

"Sure, I'm fine, just hot and tired—and maybe a

little anxious."

She had slept a few hours during the night when they dimmed the cabin lights, but twenty hours of flight time would leave anyone tired. At least she was talking more now.

"What did you think of your first airplane flight?"

"Oh," she began, her eyes widening as she turned to look at him, "I thought it was exciting, although long." Then she frowned. "The plane looked huge from the outside, but I only counted twenty-four seats. It was a lot smaller inside than I'd imagined."

"Really?" He'd never thought about it, just taken the size for granted.

She nodded. "It felt like they'd packed us in that cabin like sardines in a can, then hurled us all into the air."

The comment took John by surprise. His deep laugh boomed out, causing the cabby to glance at them in the mirror.

"I gotta say, I was impressed by the air stewardess, though. She looked very nice in her uniform. But can you imagine having a job like that where you have to be a nurse, no taller than five-foot-four, no more than one-hundred and eighteen pounds, and single? I qualify." She chuckled. "Except the nurse part, so I guess I won't be applying to work for the airlines."

"That's good. I'd hate for you to be gone all the time, flying all over America." He smiled, remembering her child-like wonder at seeing clouds up close. He'd gotten to see everything from a different point of view while seated next to Hannah.

The uneventful flight, even with landing for fuel five times and taking off again, had helped settle her nerves, but if her widened eyes were any indication, the taxi ride to the hotel had wiped away any chance of calm. Instead, it had apparently renewed her fears—maybe even her doubts about coming.

He couldn't begin to imagine her thoughts at the moment, but growing up believing her father was dead and now getting closer and closer to meeting him for the first time must be wearing her nerves to a frazzle. He wanted to assure her everything would be fine, but they would both know his words were empty promises. He settled for taking her hand. Only a much higher power knew how the meeting would go.

A loud horn drew his attention and held it while two drivers exchanged opinions of each other in a shouting match. Tempers seemed to be as hot as the heat rising up from the sun-baked asphalt.

Beside him, Hannah frowned and stared down at their linked hands, her mind probably conjuring up scenes of murder and mayhem like the sensational stories plastered on the big screen where she worked, or the newspaper headlines. He didn't blame her for being nervous; he only hoped she didn't hate him when the day was over.

She twisted in the seat to face him, sliding her hand from his and clamping her fingers around his wrist. "This is a mistake. I never should have come."

Her short nails dug in, surely leaving crescent dents in his skin, but his focus was on the look of terror that had transformed her face. Her eyes constricted even as he noticed a movement of one hand lifting to cover her stomach.

"There's no need to panic," he told her, keeping his voice low and calm. "You have nothing to fear. *You're* the one in control here," he assured her. "He's the one on trial, not you."

"If I'm in control," she whispered, eyeing the back of the driver's head, "why is my heart pounding so hard and the blood rushing past my ears so loud I can hardly hear my own voice?"

She removed her hands and sat back against the seat. Her posture reminded him of a plank of wood.

"Honey, we've come all this way. He's waiting for you—for us. I'm right here with you. Just remember, he may be your father, but you don't owe him anything."

"But he's a *mob boss*—a criminal," she hissed out between gritted teeth, her voice barely above a whisper to keep the cabby from overhearing.

Her eyes closed and her hands clenched into fists. As if praying for strength to face the enemy, her lips moved, but no sound came out.

A remembered Sunday school story about David versus Goliath came to mind. *Yes, Vince would probably seem like a real life Goliath to her.*

Whatever her divine request, it must have been granted as her shoulders slowly relax, and she eventually opened her eyes.

"Hannah," he said, then frown slightly as he brought her cold hands to his lips. "Your hands are like ice." He rubbed them between his as he continued. "Listen to me. You are strong. Stand up to him. He cares about you—deeply. He won't push you. You've kept a lot of your feelings to yourself about having a father, but I doubt he'll try to change your mind. He'll leave it up to you to accept or reject him."

"How can you be sure about that unless you're one of his...one of...*them*."

Her words hissed out with force, hitting their mark like a slap to the face. "No!" John reached for her hands, but she withdrew, clutching them both together in her lap; her lips tightened into a thin line. "No," he repeated, his voice a hoarse whisper. "I'm *not* connected with him." Even without raising his voice, his frustration sent the words out with anger-driven force and conviction. "I flew to Los Angeles from Mobile, Alabama, *not* from New York."

She no longer cowered. In fact, she slowly raised her chin an inch and narrowed her eyes to glare at him. "You're right. I don't owe my father anything—and the more I think about it, I don't owe *you* either."

He frowned at this turn of her character. "What are you talking about?"

"You've spied on me, lied to me, and now I have a feeling you're leading me right into the viper's den. What have you gotten me in to?" Without waiting for an answer, she turned back to stare straight out the side window of the taxi, arms crossed and face tight.

Where had the anger at him come from? He never pushed her to visit Vince—only suggested. She had made up her own mind. Was she blaming him now because she was unhappy with her choice? Was this just her anxiety talking?

John closed his eyes and concentrated on breathing normally. He'd already lost too much sleep worrying about Vince's reaction when they arrived. Sure, he'd betrayed the man's trust by divulging everything to Hannah, but would his breach of family loyalty be overlooked since the man would finally get to see and talk with his daughter in person? Men had been eliminated for not being loyal. Although he wasn't afraid of Vince going to that extreme, heaven only knew how big a hornet's nest he was walking into.

What have I gotten us both into?

"Here we are folks. The Ritz."

John jerked his thoughts back and reached across to squeeze Hannah's cold hands as the taxi pulled to the curb.

He reluctantly let her go to step out and around to the back of the vehicle. Pulling out his wallet, he glanced up to find the fare was being handled by a familiar young man in a black suit.

The gentleman then offered Hannah a hand to steady her as she stepped from the taxi. "Good afternoon, ma'am. How was your flight?"

The smile she flashed the don's driver gnawed at his stomach; she didn't realize the man was part of Vince's organization.

The driver merely nodded toward him, then turned to lead them into the hotel lobby. John knew the drill, but he hadn't thought to tell Hannah. When they exited into the alley, she frowned, glancing around until she met his gaze with a fearful one of her own.

"What's going on?"

"Honey, everything is fine. I'll explain what's taking place once we're in the car, but right now, we need to hurry."

"Ma'am," the young man said, opening the back door of the sedan and offering her a hand.

Her eyes narrowed slightly even as her jaw firmed and her nostrils flared. She stood with one hand planted firmly on a hip, shifting her glare between the lackey holding the passenger door and him. "I asked you a question—one I think deserves an answer."

When the young man began to blink rapidly and look around, John took pity on him and put a hand on Hannah's back. "It's safe. I promise. Please, just get in the car. They'll drive us to where he is."

"Are you sure? They look—"

"I'm sure," he assured her quickly.

Thankfully, after a huff, she climbed into the back seat, ducking her head to get the wide-brimmed hat inside without incident. He joined her, sliding up close and leaning over to speak in a lowered voice. "Vince feels it's safer for us to arrive at a hotel, and safer for him to have us meet at his home where he can better guard us and the situation."

Those blue eyes darkened in concerned again, and her breathing became shallow as she processed the explanation. The car lurched forward, momentarily pinning her back in the seat, but she managed to nod.

She remained silent en-route to Vince's compound. John had no way of knowing what was going through her mind, but she probably wished she could go back in time and make a different decision.

When the car turned off the highway and raced up the long, curved driveway, she reached over and slipped her hand into his. When he turned his head, their gazes connected. As if picking up a precious vase, he gently lifted the trembling hand, bringing her chilled fingers to his lips. He recognized fear tensing her body, but knowing she trusted him enough to turn to him in her stress made all the difference in his confidence to stand up to whatever Vince's reaction would be.

They were a united force facing the enemy together.

Once inside the tall, rod-iron gate, John moved a

few inches to the side and pointed out the window. She leaned forward and caught her first glimpse of the huge house perched on top of the hill. He had to smile when her jaw relaxed and lips parted.

"Goodness, gracious," she whispered. Then she blinked several times and glanced around as if wondering who might have heard her expression of astonishment.

When he smiled at her, she sat up straighter, pulled her hand from his, and clamped her lips together.

He grinned at her child-like innocence...and stubbornness. *Charming.*

When the sedan stopped just inside a second double gate, John stepped out and offered a hand to assist Hannah from the car before he guided her toward the fortress-sized front entrance.

"That door looks like it belongs on a castle, and is definitely strong enough to keep out the Trojan army," she noted, keeping her voice low. "Where's the moat and drawbridge?"

He chuckled, flashing back to his favorite childhood book about King Arthur and the Knights of the Round Table.

The driver stepped around them and knocked once, then three times before he unlocked and opened the door, stepping aside to usher them inside.

The foyer was dark and cavernous, echoing their footsteps as they crossed to the archway leading into the living room. He saw her shiver.

"Don't be nervous," he said under his breath. "He's just a man."

"Sure," she mumbled, glancing up from under the brim of her hat just before she slipped it off and held it between them. "And this is just another day in the park with the pigeons and the kiddies, right? I didn't ask for this. I just wish I knew for sure whose side you're on. For all I know, he paid you to get me here and—"

"No." He shook his head. "I'm here for *you*. Right here beside *you*."

She firmed her lips and turned toward the living room. The opposing team had just arrived, and the ball game was about to begin.

Hannah felt out of place. This house was bigger than the entire boardinghouse of eight apartments. The massive entry featured a heavy, dark-wood table with a huge vase of cut flowers artfully arranged. A crime boss with flowers in his entry didn't fit the stereotype she'd read about.

Of course, neither did the man when he walked up to greet them. She held her breath. He wore black slacks and a white shirt with both sleeves rolled to the elbows.

Ordinary.

What had she expected? Horns and a pitchfork? Or a pool-hall atmosphere where men sat around drinking beer and smoking cigarettes? With his hair receding a little bit and slim and trim build, this man looked like any other father in the world.

Her stomach clenched, squeezing like a vice and holding her rooted to the spot for fear her legs would buckle. The slight tightening of John's hand reminded her of his presence, his encouragement. Surely, he'd catch her if she faltered.

"Come in, come in." Vince Giovanni spoke as if to them both, but his eyes never moved from her.

She trembled inside, a death-grip strangling the

clutch-purse at her side.

"You look just like your mother," he murmured before shaking his head and motioning for them to take a seat on the sofa.

Hannah released the held breath, thankful he hadn't tried to hug her.

After a moment's hesitation, she moved forward, but silence hovered over the small group as she set her hat and purse on the end of the sofa and took a seat.

John sat beside her, and Vince took the chair across from them. He then cleared his throat, and took the lead. "Drinks will be served in a moment. Is lemonade okay?"

She nodded, wishing she could be sure her voice would be strong when she eventually had to speak.

"How was the flight?"

"Uneventful, but long." The words came out with less volume than she would have liked.

"Yes, that's a rough trip." He nodded, his gaze still uncomfortably glued to her. "Um…" He blinked several times before he leaned back and crossed his legs. "I'm sorry for staring, but your resemblance to Sadie is amazing. The shape of your eyes and the hair. Even your sense of style brings back fond memories. Your mother was beautiful and loved nice clothes and shoes."

His words touched a soft spot, but she steeled her emotions. "Why did you never come visit my mother? Us?" She swallowed. Okay, blurting out her number one question was rather rude, but her voice, although soft, had remained steady and direct.

Thank goodness.

Vince lowered his gaze to stare at his own hands;

hands that had, no doubt, taken more than a few lives; ones that were a larger version of her own, complete with a uniquely curved baby finger on his right hand. If nothing else, that one trait would have convinced her of his role in her birth.

Finally, he heaved a deep sigh and met her gaze. "I never thought this day would come. I thought I'd made it clear," he continued, shifting his attention momentarily toward John, "that you were never to know about me. Never to be put in possible danger. Some people don't listen, don't use their heads."

The cold glare he pinned on John sent another shiver down her spine. What would he do to him for telling her? She glanced his way, but he appeared relaxed.

When her father spoke again, it drew her attention back to him.

"At the time your mother left, the organization— the family—was in turmoil with our don having just been…eliminated. I moved up the ranks to replace him. There were others who thought I was too young and lacked the experience to get things done, so we were busy. They were wrong to think I couldn't handle the position I'd filled."

At the sight of Vince's jaw clenched, lips mashed into a straight line, and eyes stormy and lethal, she recoiled slightly, pushing back into the cushioned sofa, and involuntarily reaching over to rest a hand on John's arm. The muscle under her hand tensed, relaxed, and then tensed again, as if sending a Morse code message that he was there for her. A sigh eased out.

While she watched, the don's hands gradually relaxed, but it took him several deep breaths before he visibly regained control. She knew nothing of what had transpired so long ago, but the incident still had power to stir his anger. Obviously, he'd never gotten over the experience—never forgiven whomever killed the former family leader. Had he gotten revenge?

That last thought made her shudder, but, surprisingly, she didn't fear Vince. She remembered John's words: *"You have nothing to fear…you don't owe him anything. He's the one on trial."* One day, either on earth or later, he'd have to answer for his crimes, but that was his problem, not hers.

"My first thought," he continued, "was to immediately find her and bring her home, kicking and screaming if necessary, and that was even before Dr. Baron told me she was expecting."

Hannah hung on every word, not wanting to feel emotional, but knowing her mother must have been scared to death that he would do exactly that—drag her back to New York. "But you didn't know where she'd gone."

"It took a week or so. A couple of my men followed the paper trail and found her. Problem was, the family—the business—was in an uproar. My lieutenant suggested I let things settle down a bit more since it still wasn't safe here. Men were sleeping all over the house and…well…" He rubbed a large hand over his mouth and glanced away for a moment before returning his gaze to her. "Anyway, I decided to wait. By the time I got things situated in my favor, you'd been born."

She leaned forward. "So, why didn't you head to California?" *But if he had, I'd have been raised a mobster's daughter.*

A shudder ran down her spine.

After sucking in a deep breath, he sighed, accepted a glass of lemonade and took a long drink while his employee handed one each to her and John.

After setting the glass on the coffee table, Vince continued. "Plans were to slip out and fly west the following week, but it was my mother's birthday. My boys brought her here for a little celebration. It didn't take her long to ask what was bothering me." He rolled his shoulders in a casual shrug. "I told her about Sadie leaving but held back the part about you. I thought it would be a nice surprise later when I got you both home."

Hannah clenched her hands in her lap to keep him from seeing them tremble. *I have a grandmother?* Her heart thudded several times while she waited for him to continue.

"I'm not sure what possessed me to bring up the subject, but I asked her what it had been like having her husband working for the mob as an enforcer." He fell silent, staring off toward the dining room.

"Is your mother still alive?" she couldn't help asking into the silence.

He eventually blinked several times, cleared his throat, and continued. "No." With only a brief hesitation, he resumed where he'd left off. "She told me about sleepless nights and the terror of never knowing if her husband would get home alive. She understood, and she was a good Italian wife, so she kept her fears to herself, telling me how several nights he arrived home bloody or shot. The doctor would be called to patch him up, and then he'd return to work."

She swallowed, forcing back unexpected tears at

the thought of anyone in her family—or John—being shot and her having to tend to bleeding wounds. Deep down, it also hurt to hear that she'd not get to meet her grandmother. "Did she ever ask him to quit?"

"No." The answer was abrupt, his face hardening for a moment. Then he shrugged and smiled. "You don't quit the family."

His features were hard, cold. Had she missed anything by not living with this man? She didn't think so. "How old were you when your father died?"

"Sixteen, but I was already on the payroll. I was too young to take over for Pop, so my uncle moved up. He had no sons, so, naturally, he groomed me to take over after him. He led the family for just over ten years."

How could these men keep doing whatever it was they did—gambling, prostitution, liquor—when it meant so many of them would die?

The thought made her stomach queasy, but she remained quiet, wondering if she really wanted to hear more of this story. Sure, she'd asked him to explain, but she'd seen a couple gangster movies; now, she suspected there was more truth in them than fiction.

"How was your mother able to handle so many of her family members getting killed? How did she live life and do all the normal things when she could lose someone else at any moment?"

"I know she lit a candle every week, asking for me to walk away from the mob, but despite being Italian, she didn't understand that even as a teen, I was already in too deep. Besides," he said, lowering his voice slightly and giving her a sly smile and a wink. "I didn't want out."

He'd *wanted* to be a thief and a murderer even as a teenager? She wasn't sure what to say to this revelation. No wonder her mother ran for her life and lied to keep her away from the man.

She tightened her grip on the glass of lemonade. Tears weren't far below the surface.

John leaned closer, touching her arm. "Are you okay?"

Hannah nodded, sliding her hand away without taking her gaze from Vince. "So, um, you said your mother lived in fear of your father dying. As a child, did you ever fear dying?"

A shrug jerked his shoulder up and down. "When I was young, before I turned twelve and my father insisted I remain with the men, there were times when my mother bundled me up and we slipped out at night to drive to my aunt's in Jersey. We'd stay there until things settled down. The families had a code of honor back then. Business was strictly between the men. Women and children were left alone. Of course, times changed, and a few scum weren't as careful about honoring the code. Anyway they could get at a don, they'd use it—even if his family was in the car and it meant killing his kids. Sad things happen occasionally." He sighed, shaking his head. "*That's* why I left you and your mother in California and just had my guy keep an eye on you. He reported back if either of you needed anything."

"I understand you own the boardinghouse and hired my mother as manager."

Vince scratched his cheek, casting a quick glare at John before relaxing the scowl and turning his attention back to her. Would this be strike two in a list of disloyal acts?

"Well, let's just say my attorney was involved in arranging an anonymous purchase. Then he chose Sadie as the manager from the applications and gave her a small salary and free rent for taking on the added responsibility. I saw the arrangement as a way for her to have a little more money available to spend on you." A sheepish shrug followed his grin. "You might call it child support."

No words got past the lump in her throat. John had told the truth. Her father, as much as she hated the thought of being a mobster's daughter, cared about her—might even love her…in his own way.

A rough-looking man of about fifty stepped into the room. He was dressed much like her father, but there was a gun strapped around one shoulder. He didn't smile, yet, to her amazement, she felt no fear. He looked just like one of the actors in the gangster movies.

"Excuse me, sir. The meal is on the table."

"Ah, good." Vince stood and led the way into the dining room. "Let's eat. Sit, sit," he urged, stopping at the end of the table and motioning for her to take the seat on his right. John took the one on the left.

Hannah swallowed once, then a second time as the smell of spicy food wafted up to clash with her already churning stomach. One way or the other, she intended to make it through the meal without showing weakness.

She blinked several times. *With that attitude, maybe I'm more like my father than I even realize.*

The next hour was spent listening to Vince tell stories about John when he was a boy. Although interesting, and even humorous at times, she was unable to eat more than a few bites of the delicious noodle dish. Her stomach revolted against each nibble. The meal couldn't be over soon enough.

"Would you excuse me for a few minutes? I need to use the ladies' room."

"Sure, sure. Straight through that doorway, down the hall, last door on the right."

She barely glanced at the hallway except to notice creamed-colored wallpaper with tiny sprigs of baby-blue flowers.

Once the bathroom door closed behind her, Hannah leaned back against the wall and closed her eyes. *I'll get through this. I will get through this.*

After another minute, she pushed away and moved to the sink, lifting her gaze to stare into the mirror. She blinked, shocked at the sunken eyes and bloodless face staring back.

Deep breaths. In, one-two-three. Out, one-two-three.

"I can do this," she whispered to her reflection as all she had learned whirled in her brain.

What if her mother had stayed? Her childhood would have been spent in this house, surrounded by men with guns always ready to defend the family. And then there was her father—the don. He looked ordinary, yet if what she'd read about the mafia was correct, he routinely broke the law and ordered people killed. What child wants someone like that for a father? What if he were arrested and sent to prison, or gunned down in the street and immortalized on the front page of every newspaper in the country?

She shook her head. As a child, she would have had no choice, but as an adult, she refused to be part of her father's life—and she would *never* allow her children to be around their grandfather. This visit answered a few questions and fulfilled an obligation, but was the first time—and last—she'd ever step foot in Vince Giovanni's home.

Her head throbbed. After running cool water over a wash rag, she patted her face, then lifted her mass of hair and ran the rag around the back of her neck, allowing it to cool her skin and settle her nerves. If she could just have a few more minutes to herself, she'd be fine. With the rag still around her neck, she sank down on the edge of the claw-foot tub and closed her eyes. Just a minute or two. That's all she needed.

****

The moment Hannah was out of sight, Vince turned to face him. "So, Johnny, I never thought you'd betray me." With a deep sigh, he settled back into the chair.

John swallowed once, knowing the confrontation wouldn't go well. He'd seen Vince use this tactic before. It would start with heaping on guilt and then move on to accusations.

Almost without conscious thought, he straightened his spine and faced the don's barely veiled anger. The man's two beefy fists rested on either side of the plate, as if poised to react if the discussion didn't go to his liking. Although he'd never agreed to that part of the man's requests, his silence had been taken for assent. There probably wasn't an acceptable excuse for going against the don's order of secrecy, but then, he didn't work for Vince and wasn't bound by such orders.

"Your demand to never tell Hannah about you put me in a position of having to lie to her, and—"

"How is it lying if you keep your mouth *shut* and don't tell her *anything*?" The man now scowled, his anger threatening to boil over.

Thinking only of Hannah, John lifted his chin a fraction and narrowed his eyes as he faced down the older man. "Her mother—Sadie—lied to her all her life by telling her about a father who died a hero. I knew the truth, yet when she first told me about this factitious man, I kept my mouth shut out of loyalty to *you*. That's called lying by omission. Your term, Vince." His own anger dripped like venom as he spat out the last words. Vince wasn't stupid. If one of his men failed to tell him of impending danger, the don would see that omission as lying. A lie was a lie, however you cut the pie.

"That doesn't change the fact you let me down, boy." His palm pressed flat against his chest. "I took you in and gave you so much when you were a kid. I love you, and then you go and break trust. You weren't loyal to me." His fist came down on the table hard enough to make the dishes bounce. "You owed me that."

"I'm sorry you feel that way, but in reality, I was *very* loyal—to myself, and the woman I've come to care about." With narrowed eyes, his glare bore into those of his opponent, meeting the challenge and standing firm, for Hannah's sake. His lips mashed together and his breathing came rapid and shallow, but he forced himself to continue. "What you gave me while I was growing up was attention, not love. Love doesn't demand anything in return." He took the napkin from his lap and laid it beside his plate. "I learned that from your daughter."

"Why did you bring her here?"

"Because Hannah *is* your daughter—your blood." He shoved back his chair. "Do you honestly think I could have dragged her here if she didn't want to come?"

A pregnant pause settled between them.

"Is something going on between you and my girl? I see how you look at her."

He swallowed, sighed. Same battle, just attacking from another angle. Was he going to play the concerned father now and demand he be asked for her hand in marriage or something?

"I won't lie to you. Yes, I'm in love with Hannah, so don't expect me to ever report to you about her. I intend to ask her to marry me in a quiet ceremony in California, and then we'll live there without interference, and where *I* will take care of her."

The frown was instant. "Are you saying you plan to marry *my* daughter *and* expect me to stay out of her life and never see her again? I've always planned to throw Hannah a big Italian wedding and, like tradition, give her and her husband their first home and car."

"First, her husband won't be just any Joe Blow, it'll be *me*." At least he prayed she'd let it be him. "And I don't need you to give us a house and car. I can take care of us. You haven't had her in your life for the first twenty-three years, so I think she and I deserve the next twenty-three to ourselves. And as to you never seeing her, that will be solely up to her. If she wants to see you every so often—fine. However," he stated, pausing for effect, "if she chooses to never see you again, I will support her decision."

The older face turned a ruddy hue and his eyes narrowed, but when the man's lips disappeared into a straight line and he lowered his chin without breaking eye contact, John knew the don was furious. There could easily be trouble—lethal trouble.

Wary of the man's temper, he forced his facial expression neutral, maintained eye contact, and waited—just like Vince had taught him. He had drawn a line in the sand by declaring his loyalty to Hannah, and now it was up to her father what the next move would be.

The don's voice had deepened, his words slow and precise. "You're saying her papa can't walk her down the aisle?"

"What I'm saying, Vince, is that it's *Hannah's* decision. But how safe would she be if you announce to the world that she's your daughter? Isn't that what this charade has been about for all these years?"

He slapped a palm over his heart, dropping back in his chair as if stricken. "Johnny, you break my heart. After what I've done for you, and now you want to kick me out of my daughter's life just when I finally get to meet her?" He shook his head. "No little grandbabies to bounce on my knee," he added, his voice gruff and slow.

John didn't relax his posture. The benevolent father and grandfather comments could easily be a ruse to get his guard down. This meeting was important, and there wasn't room for misunderstands. He knew how the man worked. At the first sign of weakness, he'd pounce, and John wanted to avoid that situation at all cost.

"Vince, you made some choices a long time ago— even in your teens—that have caused some long-term ripples in the water. Unfortunately, we all have to live with the consequences of all our decisions." He of all people understood that now.

The don's face relaxed as he apparently pondered what had been said. His gaze dropped to his plate and remained for several moments before raising. "Johnny, you're a good boy. You've done your mama proud."

It hurt to watch Vince have to admit, even if only to himself, that he had made mistakes with his daughter and would now have to pay a high price for those decision. The older man scratched his cheek, then sighed, nodding slightly as if having come to a decision.

"Johnny Boy, you've grown up a lot, and I'm proud of you. It comes as a bit of a surprise about you and my girl, but I think I'm okay with your plans. I actually hope you two do get married—she could do a whole lot worse."

The don's approval was appreciated, even if the comment about Hannah doing "a whole lot worse" was a little backhanded and humorous, but he kept his expression neutral.

"So, with that in mind, there's something you need to know about." He settled back in the chair before he continued. "When I found out where Sadie had moved, I set up a blind corporation to buy the boardinghouse and had her name put on as co-owner. Sadie never knew because my accountant got all the paperwork, but at least she'd have something if anything happened to me. Then I saw to it she became manager. After Sadie died, I made sure things were legal for Hannah to own the building outright, with my accountant in a Trustee capacity."

John was stunned. "You're saying Hannah already owns the boardinghouse and just doesn't know it?"

Vince nodded. "Yes. The rents she collects each month go into a savings account that has been growing ever since I bought the property. She's quite a wealthy woman."

John was speechless. His assumption that Vince owned it was totally wrong. How would Hannah feel about her father giving her a home and a business all rolled up in one? If she no longer wanted to live there, she'd probably be able to sell the building and live wherever she wanted...but that was a decision for another time.

Vince was silent, drinking his tea, apparently finished with his revelation.

The future was truly now in Hannah's hands, starting with whether or not she'd allow her father in her life. Of course, that also included her answer to John's own plan of asking her to marry him. He had no way of knowing what her answer would be. For all he knew, she wouldn't be able to forgive and forget his part in keeping the truth from her, even though for only a few months, and after the meeting today...

He glanced up when she walked back into the room and quietly returned to her chair.

"Are you feeling okay?"

"I'm fine. Just a slight upset stomach."

There was no missing her pale face and hesitant movements. She truly didn't feel well.

He stood. "Then why don't we get going? There's a schedule to keep. We don't want to miss our plane."

She glanced from him to her father and then back again. "Fine."

Vince frowned, but stood and walked to the door beside his daughter.

Once there, Hannah hesitated, then turned toward her father. "Thank you for allowing me to meet you."

"Same here. It was good to see you in person instead of a picture every few years. They don't do you justice," he added. "You're a beautiful young woman, and I'm proud of you. Your mama did a good job." He raised a hand, as if to touch her, then halted the movement in midair when she lifted her chin an inch and visibly leaned away. He allowed his arm to relax back to his side. "I wish you the best."

She nodded, then gave John a tentative smile when he placed an arm around her shoulders.

"Take care, Vince."

"Take care of my bambino, Johnny. There ain't nowhere in the world you can hide if…"

"Yeah, I know," he interrupted. "Good-bye."

John wondered if his suggestion for this little family reunion had been such a good idea. Would Vince force his way into their lives in the future?

He heaved a deep sigh as the driver got out to open the rear door and assist Hannah into the backseat. One way or the other, Vince would sleep in the bed he'd made for himself.

Chapter Eighteen

After being dropped off at the hotel, John guided Hannah just inside the door, hesitating until the sedan drove away before turning to link their hands. "Look, I knew we'd both be emotionally and physically exhausted after the flight and the meeting today, so I arranged for two rooms. Our plane leaves first thing tomorrow morning.

She sagged against him. "Thank you."

He smiled and turned to lead her toward the counter in the lobby.

"May I help you, sir?"

"Yes. Two rooms for John Staples."

After following the bellboy up the elevator to the fifth floor, he slipped a tip into the young man's hand and thanked him. He then followed Hannah into her room, smiling at the sight of her standing in the middle, slowly turning in a circle with her mouth hanging open and her wide-eyed stare taking in all the details.

"I never imagined a room as nice as this," she whispered, slipping off her hat and tossing it on the bed before turning to look at John. An excited laugh slipped out. "I can't believe I get to stay here tonight."

He watched her hair flare out as she twirled in a circle to take in her surroundings and ached to run his fingers through the silken length. But he held back, unsure how she'd react. Just seeing her joy was worth spending a week's salary for the rooms.

"It's like a dream." She turned to point upward. "I mean, look at the designs on the ceiling and the chandelier. And the Queen Ann sofa, bed, and desk. And the gold brocade bedspread," she continued, running a hand across the textured material draped over the foot of the bed. "It's straight out of a Paramount movie set. Beautiful. Thank you. I was dreading the thought of boarding a plane again right away."

"I knew we'd need time to relax and rest." Everything from her drooping shoulders to her fidgeting hands told him she needed something to hold on to. "Come here," he coaxed, taking her hand and leading her a step closer until he held her within his arms. "I'm sorry. Vince cares, believe me, but he doesn't know what to do, what to say, to a grown daughter." He rubbed his cheek against her silky hair, breathing in the essence that would always be his Hannah.

Unintelligible words were mumbled against his shirt.

"What'd you say?"

She turned her head a fraction. "He's not my father."

"But honey…"

"Oh, I know." She stepped back, bringing a tear-filled gaze up to connect with his. "I mean, I can't accept that cold, heartless man as my father. I now understand why my mother lied to me."

"She tried to protect you."

Hannah nodded. "And you were right. If the truth had to come out, I'm glad it happened before his enemies killed him."

He frowned, opened his mouth, but she raised a hand to stop him.

"Meeting him has made it easy to walk away. If I'd never met him and then found out the truth when he was no longer alive, I'd always have wondered."

"Walking away is your choice, but...are you doing it out of spite?"

Her forehead creased with concentration. "No. I'd say I'm more resigned to not having a father in my life. It's like you once said about having nothing to lose by asking for something. I grew up always wishing I had a dad like everyone else. In spite of having a mom, there was a piece missing—like the future was a dark tunnel without a light at the end. There was a void, a hole with nothing to fill it because he was dead." She glanced out the large window overlooking the city, taking a few moments before continuing. "Now, I know that was all lies, and I've met my father. But to expect a man like Vince to fill that void is like grasping in the dark for something that isn't there. I grew up wanting love—you know, warmth and security—but the man is cold. Impersonal." She took a deep breath and released it slowly, meeting his gaze with her normal poise and calm that always impressed him. "I'll admit that finding out my father was alive knocked me off my feet, but I had a choice to make, and *I* made it. I came, I saw. Now I know. It's enough."

"Enough?"

She shrugged. "Oh, I'll admit to a couple sleepless nights, but then once I met him, I came to realize nothing had really changed. I grew up fine without a father, and I'll continue on without one. I've lost nothing."

"You don't plan to see Vince again?"

She shook her head. "There's no need."

Her smile was weak and slow in taking hold, but he admired her handling of a difficult situation. He hadn't missed her red-rimmed eyes when she returned to Vince's table. The ordeal had been an emotional roller-coaster, but she was dealing with it far better than he expected.

"Do you think you can ever forgive Vince for not being in your life when you needed him the most?"

The shrug barely moved her shoulders. "I'll eventually forgive him for everything, like I've already forgiven my mother. I can see why she didn't want me growing up and being associated in any way with that lifestyle. If I were a mother—and someday I hope to be—I'd feel the same about my children. He can follow them from a distance like he did me—I can't stop him—but I won't allow him to be involved in their lives."

She was a truly remarkable woman. "I understand. And thank you for being kind to Vince while you were there."

"I don't agree with his lifestyle, but he gave me life. He's my birth father, so I owed him at least the respect due a father."

"He gave you more than that."

Her forehead creased, a frown erasing the calm facade.

"I was wrong before, but I recently found out who *really* owns the boardinghouse."

She frowned. "Who?" When he remained silent, she drew back and repeated. "Who?"

"You do."

"No, that can't be," she countered, slowly shaking her head from side-to-side.

"'Fraid so. Vince confirmed it and told me he'd bought it for Sadie. After her death, he put it solely in your name."

Her mouth opened, then closed while she shook her head in denial. "All the years of scrimping and saving...and it belonged to us the whole time?"

"Yep. Apparently, he kept the corporation on the paperwork as the contact—the manager—but not as owner."

"I can't believe it. That's so much to take in," she whispered, her gaze dropping to her clenched hands. Then she lifted her chin until her gaze met his. "I wonder if mother ever knew. The whole thing is so strange." When he only shrugged, she added, "I'm not sure how to feel."

"I know. I learned recently about some things he did for my own mother to be sure she would be okay, not to mention his paying for my college."

"I guess he's not all bad—at least when it comes to those he cares about."

"True, but he uses people. He used me, or tried to use me to spy on you. He called it keeping an eye on you to be sure you're safe."

He stood with his arms around her, gently swaying for several minutes.

"Honey, can you forgive me?"

Her eyes widened as she leaned back to stare up into his gaze. "Of course. You didn't do anything— although I thought so for a while," she admitted with a gentle laugh.

He chuckled when she blushed. "You honestly

thought I was one of them?"

"Yes. I thought you were his employee. I thought he'd sent you to take me back there." Her gaze momentarily dropped, then her lips mashed together. "Sorry."

"At least you know better now."

"Do I?"

His body stiffened and he scrunched his brows until her laughter filled the suite.

"Just kidding. Yes, I know better…now."

"When you left the room, I had the opportunity to set the record straight with Vince about the future."

"You told him you never intend to be part of his organization?"

"No, he already knew that." When she remained silent, waiting for him to continue, he stepped back and reached for her hands. "No, I told him I'm in love with you and intend to marry you."

Her eyes widened and her jaw went slack. Had his love really come as such a surprise?

John went down on one knee and squeezed her hands as he gazed up into her eyes. Her hands trembled, but she didn't pull away. "Hannah Montgomery, will you be my wife for as long as we both live?"

She blinked several times, but remained silent. His heart thundered. Had he misread her responses to him? Several seconds ticked by slowly while he fought the urge to speak—to beg, if necessary.

Then a smile slowly spread across her face. "Yes, John Staples, I'd be honored to marry you."

Relief washed through his body as he matched her smile and rose without releasing her hands or the gaze that held his captive. His heart swelled when she stepped into his embrace, sliding her arms around his waist and laying her head against his chest. This was where he wanted her forever—held close to his pounding heart.

He kissed her hair, breathing in the fragrance that was hers alone. When she lifted her head, he leaned in to brush a soft kiss on her lips, but one wasn't enough. His heart rate spiked when she slid her arms up his chest to circle his neck and pull him closer, deepening the kiss.

That's when he realized her whole body was trembling. "Honey, what's the matter?"

"It all seems too good to be true—and I don't want to lose you."

"Why would you ever lose me?" He tried to make eye contact, but she stared down at his shirt, a hand coming up to run a fingernail around one of the buttons.

"Look," he interrupted, again refusing to allow her to pull away. "I know you've lost people in your life that you loved, but you don't have to worry about losing me. Honey, I've loved you almost from the start. When you looked up from the spaghetti at your feet and focused on me, it was like a bolt of lightning hit me. I knew you were different, and before long, I knew I wanted you in my life forever. But, I also knew a relationship needed to be built on solid ground— honesty and mutual respect. That couldn't happen for us as long as there were secrets."

He took a deep breath, thankful she was listening and not pulling away.

"I had to find a way to convince you how much I cared," he continued, "hoping you wouldn't kick me out of the boardinghouse and out of your life when I told you the truth about my ill-fated promise to keep an eye on you. Hannah, I want us to share everything." He lifted his hands up to hold her face between his palms. "The ups and the downs, the sad things in life and the happy times. I know we can make a great life if we stand together, as a united force against the world. I'll always be here to support and protect you," he reminded her, gazing intently into her eyes. "And also to stand beside you in whatever you want to achieve in life. I love you so much."

He ran a thumb across her lips before leaning in to brush another kiss across them. When he leaned back and moved his hands down to grasp hers, she smiled, easing his mind.

"Honey, please believe me, I know you've been through a lot, but I'm not sorry this whole series of events has brought you and me together." John glanced at their joined hands. "I wasn't looking for anyone when I moved to Los Angeles. I was totally focused on the new job at Hughes Aircraft. I didn't feel empty or lost or incomplete—until I met you. You filled a hole in my life—filled a need I didn't even realize existed. Now, I can't imagine life without you in it. I can't imagine getting up each day without sharing life's ups and downs with you. I can't imagine going back to eating meals I've tried to cook," he added with a sheepish grin. Her tender smile gave him courage to continue. "I love you so much and want to spend the rest of my life making you happy."

"And designing planes," she added, broadening her smile.

"Yes, and that, too, but you're more important to me than a job. I want to marry you, have a family with you, and grow old together. I betrayed your trust once, but that will never happen again. I hope you can forgive me." He squeezed her hands, hoping she believed him—praying she felt the same. The seconds dragged by as he held her gaze.

Hannah finally stepped in closer, rose up on her toes, and kissed him. "Yes, I forgive you. I'll admit my life was turned upside down when you told me about my father—and consequently about my mother's lies. I felt as if truth had taken a flight to the other side of the world. I wasn't sure what to believe or what the future would bring. I was lost and struggling to find some balance."

"Ah, honey, I'm so sorry you had to go through this," he told her, squeezing her within his arms.

"Well, it's history now. Thank you for loving me enough to stand up to the opposition." She lowered her chin a fraction, then glanced up at him from beneath long lashes. "I've loved you for some time now, too, but never more than at this very moment. I hope you'll still love me when we're old and gray," she added with a smile, "because I love you more than I ever imagined loving someone."

"Hannah, I love you more with each breath I take," he countered, leaning in to brush his mouth across hers.

"John, I'll love you only, now and forever."

Her hands reached up to hold his face as she pressed in, meshing their lips in a way that sent fireworks exploding behind his eyelids. His dreams were coming true.

A word about the author…

Sandra McGregor was challenged by her husband in 2001 to not wait until retirement in 2005 to start writing the books he had been hearing about for decades. Picking up the gauntlet he threw down, she spent the next eight years honing her craft and finishing twenty-one manuscripts before her first sell.

She now lives in southern Georgia with her husband and cat and enjoys reading, traveling, and hearing from her readers.

http://SandraElzie.com